Amy Cross is the author of more than 250 horror, paranormal, fantasy and thriller novels.

OTHER TITLES BY AMY CROSS INCLUDE

1689
American Coven
Angel
Anna's Sister
Annie's Room
Asylum
B&B
Bad News
The Curse of the Langfords
Daisy
The Devil, the Witch and the Whore
Devil's Briar
Eli's Town
Escape From Hotel Necro
The Farm
Grave Girl
The Haunting of Blackwych Grange
The Haunting of Nelson Street
The House Where She Died
I Married a Serial Killer
Little Miss Dead
Mary
One Star
Perfect Little Monsters & Other Stories
Stephen
The Soul Auction
Trill
Ward Z
Wax
You Should Have Seen Her

BLOOD OF THE LOST

THE HORRORS OF SOBOLTON BOOK NINE

AMY CROSS

This edition
first published by Blackwych Books Ltd
United Kingdom, 2024

Copyright © 2024 Blackwych Books Ltd

All rights reserved. This book is a work of fiction. Names, characters, places, incidents and businesses are the product of the author's imagination or are used fictitiously. Any resemblance to actual persons, living or dead, or to actual events or locations, is entirely coincidental.

Also available in e-book format.

www.amycross.com
www.blackwychbooks.com

CONTENTS

PROLOGUE
page 15

CHAPTER ONE
page 23

CHAPTER TWO
page 31

CHAPTER THREE
page 41

CHAPTER FOUR
page 49

CHAPTER FIVE
page 57

CHAPTER SIX
page 65

CHAPTER SEVEN
page 73

CHAPTER EIGHT
page 81

CHAPTER NINE
page 89

CHAPTER TEN
page 97

CHAPTER ELEVEN
page 105

CHAPTER TWELVE
page 113

CHAPTER THIRTEEN
page 121

CHAPTER FOURTEEN
page 129

CHAPTER FIFTEEN
page 137

CHAPTER SIXTEEN
page 145

CHAPTER SEVENTEEN
page 153

CHAPTER EIGHTEEN
page 161

CHAPTER NINETEEN
page 169

CHAPTER TWENTY
page 177

CHAPTER TWENTY-ONE
page 185

CHAPTER TWENTY-TWO
page 193

CHAPTER TWENTY-THREE
page 201

CHAPTER TWENTY-FOUR
page 209

CHAPTER TWENTY-FIVE
page 217

CHAPTER TWENTY-SIX
page 225

CHAPTER TWENTY-SEVEN
page 233

CHAPTER TWENTY-EIGHT
page 241

CHAPTER TWENTY-NINE
page 249

CHAPTER THIRTY
page 257

EPILOGUE
page 265

BLOOD OF THE LOST

PROLOGUE

AS SOON AS SHE opened her eyes, she knew she'd done it again.

Staring up at the ceiling fan, which wasn't even running, Penelope Chandler could already feel the dull thud of a headache. She blinked, and her eyes felt sore as she began to sit up. Looking around the stuffy and dimly-lit room, she saw her boots over by the door while her suitcase had been knocked off the stand and lay on the rug with its contents spilled out across the floor. As for her clothes, they were still very much on her body, although the front of her dress was caked in some kind of stale alcohol and – as a result – was sticking to her skin.

Turning to look the other way, she saw that

the door to the bathroom was open, and it was at that moment that she began to notice a faintly sickening smell. She blinked a couple more times, still trying to get her head straight, but the only sound she heard at first were her own tired breaths.

"Hello?" she said cautiously, fully aware that this wouldn't be the first time that she'd woken up with unexpected company. "Is anyone there?"

She waited, but she heard no response and after a few seconds she let out a relieved sigh.

"Okay, so you didn't disgrace yourself quite that much," she murmured. "That's a small blessing, at least."

As she hauled her hungover body off the bed, she felt a little unsteady on her feet but she managed to begin the slow shuffle to the bathroom. At that moment she spotted her underwear on the floor, and she could only assume that in her drunken state she must have at least *tried* to get undressed for bed. She remembered going to a bar in this rundown little town, just to get some food before heading back to the motel, and she knew that – as always – she'd promised herself that she was only going to have one zero-alcohol beer before retiring to her room to get some paperwork done. One beer. She remembered being so firm about that; she remembered truly believing that this time she was going to have some discipline.

Instead, she'd made the same mistake she always made.

Feeling distinctly queasy, she reached the bathroom door and saw that evidently she'd vomited up much of the alcohol during her return the previous night. The bathroom was a complete mess, with towels everywhere and vomit in both the sink and the toilet. Horrified by the terrible state of the room, she let out a faint groan before heading to the toilet and giving it a quick flush. She began to pull her dress off, hating the familiar sensation of half-dried fabric peeling away from her skin. The dress stank of cheap booze and, for some reason, cigarettes; although she didn't smoke, she figured that she must have 'made friends' with some people who did, and she could only cringe as she wondered what her drunk self had said.

When she was sober, Penelope barely said a word to anyone, especially not to strangers. She'd been raised to only speak when she was spoken to. But when she'd had a few drinks, she could – as her grandmother had once told her – talk the hind legs off a donkey.

She tossed her dress into the shower, figuring that she'd rinse it in a moment, and then she looked at her reflection in the mirror. Her hair was matted and disheveled, her eyes were a little sore and reddened, and as she tilted her head slightly she saw a bruise forming on her cheek. The worst part was that she'd had far worse drunken adventures over the years and, despite the general air of disaster, she was actually relieved that nothing else seemed to have happened. And most importantly, she'd woken up alone, so at least there wasn't the added embarrassment of having to -

Suddenly she heard her phone ringing somewhere in the room, although the sound was strangely muffled.

"Damn it," she muttered as she headed back through.

For a few seconds, she had no idea where her phone might have been left. She picked up cushions and pillows, trying to trace the source of the noise, but so far the phone was managing to remain elusive. She tripped on her boots, almost falling, as she hurried around to the other side of the bed, yet somehow the ringing sound seemed to be everywhere and nowhere all at once. And then, just as she was starting to give up hope, she spotted a faint flashing light inside one of her boots.

Crouching down, she reached inside and pulled the phone out. She had no idea how the phone had ended up in there, but any concerns in that department were quickly forgotten as she looked at the screen and saw the name of Scottie Mendelson flashing on the screen. Although she briefly considered letting the call ring out, after a few seconds she tapped to answer and turned around, leaning against the side of the bed as she tried to pull herself together.

"Hello?" she said, hoping against hope that she didn't sound too awful. "Scottie, good morning, how are you doing?"

"Long time, huh?" he replied over the line. "How are things going at your end?"

"Same old, same old," she admitted. "I'm just on the road at the moment, sorting some things out in one of our offices here in the middle of nowhere."

"Yeah, I remember you mentioning that," he told her, before pausing for a moment. "You're not that far from Sobolton, are you?"

"From where?"

"It's this town I did some secondment work at a while back," he continued. "I was helping out Maurice Fuller, he was a medical examiner in the area. Anyway, that's not the point. The point is, I'm in Wichita now of all places, but I got wind of some strange calls about Sobolton."

"Strange in what way?" she asked.

"It might be nothing," he replied. "In fact, I really hope that it's a big fat waste of time, but... a few people have got in touch, saying that they can't contact anyone in Sobolton."

"Have they tried the sheriff's office there?"

"That's the strange part," he explained. "From what I can tell, the same thing keeps happening over and over. People make an initial report claiming that they can't contact this or that friend or relative in Sobolton, but then they stop caring. They just give up. Meanwhile delivery trucks are turning around, and the drivers can't quite explain what happened when they get back to their depots. And when I contacted some ISPs, I was told that even internet traffic seems to be somehow getting bounced back."

"What do you think's going on?" she asked.

"I have no idea," he admitted, "but I know the place and... Sobolton's got a weird atmosphere. There's something not right about the place, and I just can't get it out of my head. You must know what I mean. Some towns, especially the smaller ones out in the middle of nowhere, have a tendency to feel pretty strange. Sobolton's like that, but on steroids." He paused. "So you're staying in Maddox right now, aren't you?"

"Just outside it," she said cautiously.

"Why?"

"Could you do me a favor?" he continued. "Whenever I try to get in touch with someone in Sobolton, the same thing happens to me. I kind of... lose any sense of urgency. The point is, I think someone needs to actually go down there and see what's going on, and since you're in Maddox, I figured you're already pretty close."

"You want me to drive to this Sobolton place and check that nothing odd's going on?"

"I'll owe you massively," he replied. "I'll buy you a drink next time we meet up."

"Yeah, I don't want to think about drinks right now," she told him, once again feeling the urge to throw up. "Text me the details and I'll head on over tomorrow. I've got some free time, so I might as well take a detour. But just *how* strange is this Sobolton place, anyway? What kind of -"

Suddenly realizing that she was about to vomit, she set the phone on the bed before rushing to the bathroom and slamming the door shut.

"Are you still there?" Scottie asked over the phone. "There's one more really important thing I need to tell you before you go to Sobolton. Hey, Nellie, are you okay?"

CHAPTER ONE

Today...

"EVERYTHING THAT HAPPENS NOW is your fault. If people hadn't been so damn quick to throw Joe out, he might still be here and Sobolton would be safe. Instead it looks like the town's on the verge of falling apart."

As he drove the cruiser out of town, John couldn't help but hear those words ringing in his head. Loretta Hicks had almost spat them out, and while at the time he'd politely dismissed her opinions... now he was starting to feel the words gnawing away at his plans. Perhaps even at his soul. He turned the wheel, steering the cruiser around a particularly tight bend, but deep down he worried that he was in no fit state to be driving at all. A moment later, as he adjusted his grip on the wheel, he suddenly realized that Cassie had been talking for a while now.

"And I said to them," she continued, "just stay where you are."

"Who?" he asked, trying to refocus.

"My folks," she replied. "I was just telling you how they were getting all antsy earlier. I sure hope they're not out here tonight, trying to follow all those other idiots who headed out of town. Or if -"

"There!" he gasped, slamming his foot on the brake pedal, bringing the cruiser to a halt in the moonlight.

Ahead, several abandoned cars lay on either side of the road, with their doors wide open. There was no sign of any drivers or passengers, however, and as John switched the engine off and opened the door he couldn't help but worry that his worst fears were coming true.

"What happened out here?" Cassie stammered, climbing out of the vehicle's other side.

Ignoring that question for a moment, since he genuinely had no clue, John reached down to check that he at least still had his gun. Not that it would be much use, since he was out of silver-tipped bullets, but he figured that some kind of weapon was better than nothing. He made his way around the front of the cruiser and began to approach the abandoned cars, and with each step he became more and more aware of the unnatural silence that even now was filling the air. He glanced at the forest on either side of the road, and to his surprise he saw no sign of movement.

"Is it the wolves?" Cassie asked. "Did the wolves get them all?"

Yet again, John had no answer so he stayed quiet. Instead he approached the nearest car and peered inside. Someone had clearly left the scene in a hurry, but there was no sign of a struggle and – to his great relief – he saw no blood. The keys were still in the ignition, and as he made his way around to the front of the vehicle he touched the hood and felt that it was still a little warm. He walked over to the next car and managed a cursory check, but in truth he was already starting to realize that these vehicles had all been abandoned in more or less the same manner. Looking straight ahead, he saw that there were no obvious obstructions in the road, so there seemed to be no reason why these cars wouldn't have been able to continue on their way, but when he looked the other way he saw heavy tire marks on the road – suggesting that the cars had all screeched to a halt.

"They went into the forest," Cassie said.

John turned and saw that she was crouching by the side of the road. He hurried over, and sure enough he saw several sets of footprints heading off between the trees.

"Why would they go into the forest?" she continued. "If *I* was scared of wolves – which to be fair, I am – I'm pretty sure the forest is the last place I'd want to go."

"Sure, if you were thinking straight," he replied, before pondering the matter for a moment as he looked out into the darkness. "But I think something might have been messing with their heads."

***

A few minutes later, pushing through the forest, John tried to keep an eye on the footprints. He knew he was taking a huge risk, and that the forest was most certainly not a safe place right now, but at the same time he had an unknown number of civilians who seemed to have headed out in the same direction and he couldn't simply leave them to their fates.

"Sir, look!" Cassie said suddenly, pointing a

little to the right.

Spotting several items on the ground, John hurried over and found a backpack with all the clothes pulled out and strewn across the forest floor. He saw more clothes up ahead, and now his mind was racing as he tried to work out exactly what must have happened. So many people had rushed out of town following Toby's performance at the town hall, but they'd had – at most – a twenty minute advantage. That was more than enough time for the wolves to make short shrift of them, but deep down John was still clinging to the belief that for now at least the wolves weren't necessarily simply going around murdering people.

Not yet.

"I feel weird," Cassie said after a moment. "Do you think it's hot out here?"

"Not particularly," he murmured, barely paying attention as he watched the trees ahead.

After a few seconds, he felt something light brushing against his foot. He looked down and saw a shirt, and then he turned to see that Cassie had begun to get undressed.

"What are you doing?" he asked incredulously.

"Just getting cool," she replied with a smile, as if this was the most normal thing in the world.

"Boy, it's hot out here. I don't -"

"It's not hot!" he said firmly, grabbing her by the sides of her arms just as she was about to unbuckle her belt. "Cassie, look at me!"

"It's boiling," she replied, and as she stared back at him she was smiling with a curiously childlike grin. Her eyes, too, seemed strange, as if she was greatly amused by whatever was happening. "Chill, John," she continued. "Has anyone ever told you that you can be a little uptight sometimes?"

"Cassie, I need you to think for a moment about where you are."

He waited, and now he could see that she was starting to understand. Furrowing her brow, she looked around, and then – glancing down – she let out a gasp of shock.

"What the -"

Pulling away, she stumbled and tripped on a tree root, landing hard on the forest floor. She'd only managed to take off her shirt so far, so John grabbed it and handed it back to her. Blushing bright red from embarrassment, she fumbled as she tried to get dressed again.

"Cassie -"

"I don't know what happened!" she blurted out.

"Like I said, they can get into your mind."

"Why am I half naked?"

"If you want to speak to H.R. about it later, I'll understand," he replied, watching as she finished redressing and got to her feet. "I'm not sure how much stock they'll put in tales of wolves bending your thoughts, though. Being an out of town department, they might not be fully onboard with our recent predicament."

"I'm so sorry," she said, still blushing and unable now to look him in the eye. "I don't know what came over me. I just felt so hot and then somehow I forgot where I was, it was like I was at a beach and I didn't care about anything." Finally meeting his gaze, she had tears in her eyes now. "Am I going to get fired?"

"No, you're not going to get fired," he replied, before turning and setting off again. "Let's just pretend it never happened and -"

Before he could get another word out, he heard a howling sound coming from somewhere nearby. He stopped, and at that moment he spotted something moving low between the trees.

"Is it them?" Cassie asked, and her voice was filled with fear now as she instinctively drew her gun. "Is it the wolves?"

John watched the moving figure, but already

something seemed very wrong... even more wrong, he began to realize, than he was expecting. He heard another howl, and then another, suggesting that there were multiple wolves ahead, yet something about these particular howls seemed very strange, almost as if...

Stepping forward again, with his gun still in its holster, John picked his way between the trees until he reached the edge of a small clearing. Finally he stopped again, and to his horror he saw a dozen or so naked townspeople from Sobolton, crawling and scrabbling around on the ground, moving on all fours as they gnashed and howled at one another. As Cassie caught up to him, John could only watch the bizarre scene as the citizens – some of whom he knew quite well – scrambled around as if they were playing some kind of childish game.

"Sheriff Tench!" Miriam Hodges laughed, looking up at him with a huge grin before letting out a brief growl. "Have you come to join in with all the fun? Are you here to play with us?"

CHAPTER TWO

Sobolton, USA – 1869...

"DID YOU HEAR SOMETHING?"

Stopping suddenly, Walter Wade looked along the barren road that led through the forest. He wasn't sure exactly *what* noise had pricked his ears, but he'd definitely heard some kind of scuffling sound and now he was no longer sure that he and his traveling companion were alone.

A moment later, catching up, Patrick Cochrane stopped next to him.

"What exactly do you think you heard?" Patrick asked cautiously.

"I don't rightly know."

"Then how do you think you heard it?"

"I can't explain," Walter continued, looking around and seeing the forest stretching out on either side of the road. "I don't like it, though."

"You say that just about every ten miles."

"And I mean it!"

"We must be nearly there," Patrick continued, adjusting the bag over his shoulder before setting off again, trudging along the road. "This looks like the start of the valley. Sobolton must be just round the corner."

"That doesn't mean we're safe," Walter said, hurrying to catch up to him. "If you think about it -"

"If you think about it," Patrick replied, cutting him off, "that means there'll be people around. How many people live in this Sobolton place, anyway? A couple of hundred? It's not that weird if some of them are out and about, especially on a hot day like this."

"I don't like it."

"You don't like anything."

"I'm just wary!" Walter continued. "Didn't you hear what they were telling us back in Maddox? Two people got robbed and murdered not far from here! You never know what you're up against these days. There are some bad, bad people around and if you want my opinion, they're only getting badder." He walked in silence for a moment, lost in thought.

"It's been turning worse since the war ended, you know. The whole country's souring. People got used to killing other people and now they've developed a taste for it."

"You didn't fight in the war, did you?"

"You know I've got a bad ankle!"

"I -"

"Don't make fun of me for my ankle! It's a real problem!"

"Take it from someone who was there at Gettysburg," Patrick replied. "No-one apart from a few madmen wants to ever kill another soul. Most of us are absolutely sick of the whole damn thing and just want to live in peace. That's why I'm out here in the first place, trying to find somewhere new. I heard about a few towns out this way, but I haven't liked any of the ones I've been to so far. I'm hoping this Sobolton place is better."

"Me too," Walter said, although he sounded a little doubtful. "All I want is a chance to make something of myself, and to be left alone by people who've got no business meddling in my affairs. Is that too much to ask?"

"It is not," Patrick said, before stopping again as he saw water in the distance, glistening beneath the hot summer sun. "And that, my friend, must be the lake. The gentleman in Maddox said that when we see the lake, we're nearly there." He turned to Walter. "Looks like we're gonna get a chance to take in this Sobolton place after all."

***

Horses whinnied and voices cried out and a carriage rumbled past, as Patrick and Walter finally reached the bottom of the sloping road and found themselves at the edge of Sobolton. A makeshift sign stood nearby, noting the population as no more than 308 souls, but a series of constant hammering sounds rang out to mark several spots where new buildings were being constructed.

"Not bad," Walter muttered, stopping next to the sign and looking around for a moment. "Not bad at all. I've got a good feeling about this town."

"Hello there," a man said, setting his tools down and wiping sweat from his brow as he stepped toward the new arrivals. "And who might you be?"

"Honest men looking for work," Patrick told him.

"Honest men looking for work are welcome here," the man replied, conspicuously looking him up and down for a moment. "If that's what you really are."

"It is," Walter said quickly.

"Where have you traveled from?" the man continued, as several others began to make their way over, forming a small but clearly very concerned welcome party.

"We just passed through a town called Maddox," Patrick explained. "Before that Taerudville and Montgomery, and before that a little place called... I don't remember the name, actually. We've been asking around, and several people told us that we should try to find our way here."

"Are you Christian men?"

"We are," Patrick and Walter both replied.

For a moment, silence fell as the townspeople continued to watch their new guests, but finally the group parted a little as an older man limped through and stopped at their head. This man – whose face was almost entirely obscured by a huge bushy white beard with matching mustache and eyebrows – seemed content for a few seconds to merely stare at Patrick and Walter, almost as if he was daring them to be the first to speak.

Walter glanced over at Patrick, already starting to seem a little nervous.

"My name," the white-haired man said finally, projecting his voice clearly, "is Ignacious Huddlestone and I'm the mayor of Sobolton. I was elected to that role one year ago, by the good people of this town, and one of my many jobs is to make sure that we keep ourselves all safe. As you can imagine, out here so far from any other settlement, we're a tight-knit community where everyone pulls together for the common good." He took a moment to clear his throat. "We work hard to maintain a thriving atmosphere here, and you'll be welcome if you show you can contribute something."

"I believe we can," Patrick told him. "I've got experience in house-building and ditch-digging, if I can be of service in either of those roles. I also -"

"He fought in the war," Walter added eagerly.

"I did indeed," Patrick continued, although he seemed a little uncomfortable with that revelation.

"And on what *side* did you fight in the war?" Ignacious asked, tilting his head back a little as if this was the only way he could properly see out from beneath his bushy eyebrows.

"It's funny," Patrick replied cautiously, "but it being a few years back now, I'm not even sure I remember."

"Good answer," Ignacious mused, before turning to Walter. "And what about you?"

"Oh, I didn't fight at all," Walter said

proudly, before waiting for a response. "That's a good answer too, isn't it?"

He waited again, before turning to Patrick.

"Isn't it?"

He turned to Ignacious again.

"I've got a bad ankle, see," he added. "It causes me real bother."

"If you're who and what you say you are," Ignacious continued, "you're both more than welcome here in Sobolton. I won't beat around the bush. Life here is hard but fair, and a hard worker will get his due. We don't tolerate foolishness, though, nor do we condone laziness. We expect you to work, and to show up at church on Sundays, but other than that we're a community of like-minded free man and women who merely want to get on with our lives. We all came out her for similar reasons, so I'm hoping you'll fit right in."

He paused again.

"If you don't, though," he added finally, "you'll be kindly expected to leave. Please don't consider that to be a result of unfriendliness, it's just how we do things around here. Many of those who've arrived here have made their homes with us, as you can see. A few, though, have eventually realized that it was best for them to get out of town. If I haven't made myself clear, then please allow me to phrase it another way. We don't want no trouble."

"You won't get any from us," Patrick told him.

"Absolutely not," Walter added keenly.

"Are you brothers or something?" Ignacious asked.

"We just met on the road," Patrick replied, "and -"

Before he could get another word out, a wolf howled in the distance. He turned and looked toward the treeline, and he listened as the howling sound petered away to nothing.

"They got wolves round here?" Walter asked. "No-one ever mentioned them having wolves round here."

"Why don't you come along with me?" Ignacious said firmly. "Everyone's mighty busy this afternoon, but I'm an old man and my laboring days are behind me."

A ripple of laughter spread throughout the gathered crowd.

"I'll show you the ropes and help you find a way to settle in," Ignacious continued, turning and starting to limp back the way he'd come, while gesturing with his right hand for the new arrivals to follow. "There's no need to be afraid," he added. "We're friendly here to people who are friendly back. Sometimes, though, it just takes a little time to figure out who's who."

Patrick and Walter glanced at one another, as if each of them had trouble quite understanding everything that had just happened.

"Let's go with the nice gentleman," Patrick said finally, before setting off through the gap in the crowd, watched by dozens of unfamiliar faces. "Greetings," he said to the others as he passed them. "You sure have a nice town here."

CHAPTER THREE

Today...

STANDING IN A CORRIDOR at the station in town, John listened to the sound of people sobbing in one of the interview rooms. He'd been in that exact same spot for a while now, scarcely able to believe everything that had occurred over the previous hour or so, but a moment later he heard a familiar set of slightly unsteady footsteps accompanied by the gentle bumping of a cane.

"What do you think of this beauty?" Doctor Robert Law asked, stopping and holding up a new wooden cane. "There's no silver tip, unfortunately, but as canes go... I'm quite happy. I was given it a while ago, but I didn't need to break it out until today."

He turned and looked over at one of the open doors, and for a moment he too listened to the sobs.

"I found twenty-two people from the town in the forest," John said darkly. "They'd stripped naked and were crawling around on all fours, acting like..."

For a few seconds, he couldn't quite bring himself to finish that sentence.

"Wolves," he admitted finally.

"Twenty-two?" Robert replied. "That's not a lot."

"We just brought them in," he continued, "and we're going to go out and check another route. I'm fairly sure that everyone who left town after Toby's speech is going to be in the same predicament." He turned to Bob. "They're toying with us. They're literally treating us like we're goddamn playthings, and right now there's nothing we can do about it."

"When Lisa and I tried to take the kid out of town," Robert replied, "the car just... rolled to a halt."

"These wolves can do things I truly don't understand."

"And that's with a well-maintained vehicle,"

Robert continued. "I don't know if I've talked to you about it much, but it's my pride and joy. I know every nut and bolt in that car, and it's in perfect condition. There's no way it'd just break down!"

"We can't escape," John told him. "That much is very clear by now. It doesn't matter what kind of supposedly clever plan anyone comes up with, the wolves are always one step ahead. They're playing relatively soft so far, but we can't assume that'll last forever. They'd biding their time but eventually they're gonna want to press the matter a little more, then a little more than that, and then -"

"And then one day they'll really lose their patience."

"Exactly, and that day can't be far off. The only way to end this madness is..."

His voice trailed away for a few seconds. Yet again, he couldn't force himself to admit the truth.

"We can't let them take that girl," Robert said firmly.

"Believe me, I know that."

"We need to make them realize that they're banging the wrong drum," he continued. "Is there any more news on that pendant? Right now, it seems like the only thing we can use against the wolves."

"We don't even know that it's still in the town," John pointed out. "All the stories about it sound more like fairy tales than actual history. I'm sure there's a grain of truth involved in the whole thing somehow, but so far we've drawn a complete blank." He paused again. "Fortunately not many people know that fact. We're certain that there's an undercover wolf in the town, something known as the Walker. It could be anyone. It could be you or me."

"I think I'd know if I was a werewolf," Robert suggested.

"There's only a very small group of people that I truly trust," John said awkwardly, "and you're most certainly one of them. But if the Walker is around, it could be someone who's been known in Sobolton for some time. From what I've heard, these spies embed themselves in the town over a period of several decades, and their sole purpose is to feed information about local events back to the wolves. For now, they clearly aren't sure whether or not we still have that pendant, but they're obviously suspicious. We need to find it while we still have a chance, and we also need to make sure that the wolves don't find out that it's definitely missing."

"How exactly do you propose that we're going to manage that?" Robert asked, and the tone of his voice suggested that he knew the task was immense.

"For the sake of argument," John continued, as more sobbing drifted through from the nearby room, "we're going to assume that the pendant *is* still here somewhere. So if someone hid it long ago, for some reason, then we need to try to work out where."

***

"Michael, stop! Get your hands off me!"

Letting out a sudden shocked gasp, Lisa sat bolt upright on the sofa. Drenched in sweat, she stared across the darkened room for a moment, unsure of her surroundings. Her heart was racing, but after just a few seconds she realized that she was in John Tench's home and that she'd been dreaming.

Leaning back, she let out a relieved sigh. Although the nightmare about being back in the cabin with Michael had felt so very real, at least it was over now.

Getting to her feet, she wiped sweat from her face, smearing it on the sleeve of her shirt as she made her way around the sofa and headed toward the bedrooms. Reaching the door to the room at the back, she heard music playing softly as she stopped in the doorway. To her immense relief, she saw that Eloise was fast asleep on the bed while the CD from Joe's garage continued to play in the room.

"So he went on down to McGinty's," a woman was singing, her voice barely audible since the volume was so low, "and he put his money down."

Stepping over to the dresser, Lisa tapped a button, shutting the music off.

"Mommy?"

Immediately stirring, Eloise turned over on the bed and looked up at her.

"Sorry," Lisa replied, already regretting her decision to intervene. "I thought you were fast asleep."

She tapped the button again, restarting the song, before making her way over and sitting on the side of the bed.

"You really like this music, huh?" she continued, as she reached out and tucked a strand of hair behind Eloise's ear. "I truly never had you down as a folk music kind of girl. At least one good thing came out of that trip to see what Joe Hicks had in his garage."

"I just like the way it sounds," Eloise replied, looking over at the CD player for a moment. "And I like her voice. And the words, too. It's like she's in the room with us now."

"I think the CD was recorded not that long ago," Lisa explained.

"But how old are the songs?"

"Some of them are probably *very* old," she said as the previous song ended and a new one began. "They were written by people who lived in this part of the world back in the day."

"They make me feel safer."

"He was a stranger in our town," the woman sang as the song got going. "He saved us from the evil, and he gave his life in turn."

"I know what you mean," Lisa admitted, before pausing for a moment to listen as the song continued. "It's weird to think about people sitting down and writing these things all those years ago. And then most of them get lost, but a few survive and eventually they're recorded like this so that -"

"Are the wolves going to get us all?" Eloise asked suddenly, as if she'd been holding that question in for quite some time.

"No," Lisa replied, shaking her head before she'd really had a chance to consider the question at all. "Absolutely not."

"How are you going to make them go away?"

"Sheriff Tench and I are coming up with a plan," she continued. "It's a secret plan, so I really can't share the details with too many people."

"Not even with me?"

"Not right now," Lisa lied, trying her best to make her daughter feel a little better. "It's one of those things where you only tell people if they really *need* to know, and you don't need to know so... I guess that makes you lucky."

"But will the wolves be gone by the morning?"

"Maybe not quite that fast, but soon."

"How soon?"

"When everything's ready," Lisa said, struggling to maintain the untruth now. "I'm sorry I have to be so mysterious about it, but you need to trust me. And trust Sheriff Tench too. The wolves can snarl and growl and howl all they want, but that doesn't mean they're going to succeed. Sometimes it's the quiet ones who turn out to have been the strongest all along. And this town has withstood the wolves for so many centuries now."

She finally managed a smile, even if she worried that it wasn't particularly convincing.

"So you see," she added, "there's no way we're going to let them hurt us now."

CHAPTER FOUR

Sobolton, USA – 1869...

"GENTLEMEN," IGNACIOUS HUDDLESTONE SAID, reaching his desk and turning just as Patrick and Walter followed him through into his office at the rear of the little wooden town hall, "I hope you don't think that I was unwelcoming out there. That was never my intention."

"We never felt that at all," Patrick replied, glancing around the rather bare room for a moment. "We've had far worse welcomes in other places."

"Truth be told," Ignacious continued, "we here in Sobolton have been facing some... challenges for a while. That's the problem when you start to build something good. Others always come along and think they can take it for themselves."

"We heard about some killings on the roads hereabouts," Patrick told him.

"Word travels fast," Ignacious admitted with little evident relish. "This town is less than two hundred years old, as far as we can make out, but its founding is a bit of a mystery. There are records of a Father Oliver Porter or Prior or something like that, who was here around the 1750s with a small following. The town damn near died out after that, but somehow it kept going and then gold was found a while back. A fair few people moved out this way, but they ended up mostly striking dirt and moving on to California. What they left behind was just enough of a town for others to build on, and we've been trying to do just that ever since. The Ringborn railroad line's coming through soon, and right now we're kinda clinging on and hoping that'll shake everything up again."

"Should do," Patrick suggested. "Railroads have a habit of that."

"Did you just say that there's gold here?" Walter asked, taking a step forward. "As in... gold that honest people could dig up out of the ground? Enough gold to make him rich?"

"If there's any left, only a madman would try to find it," Ignacious told him. "We're trying to build more on things that we can see already. This is good land, we have a lot of resources and I might be biased but I'm confident that we can make it on our own, at least until that railroad reaches us. But like I told you, there are bandits around who think they can take whatever they want."

"Have you organized to try to stop them?" Patrick asked.

"We've tried, but they're organized too and we haven't had much luck. That's why a few of us were worried that you two fellows might be connected to them."

"We're not," Patrick said firmly.

"I believe you," Ignacious told him. "For now, you're welcome to stay here and we can even find you somewhere to sleep while you make something for yourselves. I'll arrange for someone a little younger than myself to show you around properly and help you make yourselves at home, and then -"

Suddenly cries rang out beyond the town hall. Patrick immediately hurried to the window and peered out; Walter and Ignacious made their way over to join him, just as several men raced past.

"Not again," Ignacious sighed, sounding utterly resigned to more bad news. "Lord, protect us from these bandits. We just want to live in peace."

***

"Another two men dead!" a voice cried out at the front of the crowd that was gathering near the makeshift wooden church. "Slaughtered near the lake for the furs they'd collected. Now the bandits are making camp a little way along the shore and we all know how this is gonna play out. They'll take and take and take, until we drive them away!"

"I thought they weren't coming back this time," a woman sobbed. "Why won't they leave us alone?"

"We'll go out there and deal with them once and for all," the man said. "Who's with me?"

A murmur of agreement rippled across the crowd, and half a dozen men hurried over to some horses that had been tied to a set of wooden posts.

"Suddenly this place doesn't seem so perfect after all," Walter muttered under his breath. "Are you sure we shouldn't keep moving and find somewhere a little safer?"

Patrick hesitated for a moment, before stepping past him and heading over to join the men.

"I'd sure like to come with you," he told them.

"Have you got a ride of your own?"

"I do not."

"You can take Lee Solter's horse over there," the man said, nodding at a horse nearby. "Lee's dead now so I don't suppose he'll be needing it much. It's a good one, the name's Blackspot and by all accounts he's in his prime."

Without stopping to make small talk, Patrick

hurried over to the horse and started untying it from the post. The other men were already starting to head out, so he knew he didn't have any time to waste; once the horse was free, he climbed up onto the saddle that had been left in place. Grabbing the reins, he took a moment to get the horse under control and to teach it who was boss now, and then he began to ride after the others.

"Should I come too?" Walter asked nervously.

"You got a horse?" Patrick replied as he made his way past.

"I don't, no."

"Then I can't see how you'll be much use."

Walter opened his mouth to reply, but Patrick was already heading away. Sighing, he realized that he probably should have found some way to be more useful, although he knew that Patrick was always the more gung ho out of the pair of them. Left standing alone beyond the edge of the crowd, Walter watched the riders disappearing along a trail that led up into the forest, and then he turned to see that several of the other men in the crowd were watching him with disapproving glares.

"Bad ankle," he stammered, hoping to explain himself. "Really bad. I'm always more use in... other ways."

A murmur of annoyance rippled across the crowd as the various members dispersed, and soon

Walter was left even more alone as he realized that he'd already made a bad first impression.

"I'd only hold them back," he continued, still hoping against hope that he could prove his point. "I've got other skills, though! I'm really quite useful once you get to know me. I'm a lot more impressive than I look. People are always saying that, so long as they give me a chance."

"Nothing'll come of this, as usual," Ignacious muttered.

Walter turned to see him standing nearby.

"It'll be the same as always," the old man continued. "They might chase the bandits out for a while, but the bastards'll be back soon enough. They go round picking on each town in turn, they cover the whole area every few months and so far there's been nothing anyone can do to stop them. They're too fast, you see. They know exactly what they're doing and how they're gonna do it, and they leave the rest of us looking like chumps."

"Do they ever come into the town itself?" Walter asked.

"They don't need to. They just wait out there for someone to stray into their path, and then they kill 'em and take whatever they can get their hands on. You and your buddy are just lucky you didn't run into them on your way here today."

"First bit of good luck I've had in a while," Walter admitted.

In the distance, gunshots began to ring out.

"Fools," Ignacious sighed. "They're nowhere near the bandits yet, they're just acting and hollering all tough in some dumb attempt to scare the bastards away. If you ask me, though, that's not how they oughta be going about things at all. They need to be subtle and quiet, and sneak up on them."

"So why don't they?"

"Bravado, mostly. Foolishness contributes too, I'd wager. I guess it makes them feel better about themselves, even if it means that they don't actually get the job done properly. You know, sometimes I worry that those bandits are laughing at us. They've been taking whatever they want for a few years now and we've never been able to stop them. The worst part is that it's the same two every time. Whenever I think we're really getting ourselves started here in Sobolton, they always show up and do more damage."

"Well..."

Walter thought for a moment, trying to work out exactly what he could say, but in truth words were already failing him.

"Maybe you'll get lucky this time," he managed finally, offering a shrug. "You never know, right? Sounds like you're overdue in that department." He looked around for a moment. "Now, did I imagine it, or did someone mention that there's a saloon here? While we wait for the others to get back, I'd sure like to meet a few of the locals and see how things work in a place like this."

CHAPTER FIVE

Today...

"WE'VE ACCOUNTED FOR PRETTY much everyone who tried to leave town last night," Cassie said as she followed John out of the station, blinking in the bright morning sunlight. "It seems like Miriam Hodges and her friends weren't the only ones who ended up crawling around like dogs. Eventually everyone sort of wandered back along the roads."

"So there were no casualties?" John asked, stopping by the side of the road and looking both ways.

"Not so far," she admitted, before pausing for a few seconds. "So that's good, right? I mean, if you think about it, those wolves could have murdered everyone out there, but they didn't."

John turned to her.

"I just mean," she continued, clearly already losing confidence in her argument, "that we could maybe... try to negotiate with them."

Before he could answer, John spotted several figures hurrying across the road and disappearing into McGinty's. He recognized some of the men as Toby's friends, and the way they walked made him worry that they were up to something serious. Already his mind was racing, and he knew that he had to deal with the challenge posed by Toby, but a moment later he heard footsteps and he turned to see Lisa and Eloise making their way along the sidewalk.

"I'm not sure you should be out in the open like this," he told them cautiously.

"We can't stay cooped up in your place forever," Lisa told him. "Besides, if the wolves were interested in snatching us off the streets, they could have tried that a dozen times over during the night. They're obviously going for a more subtle approach, so we should take advantage of that fact by focusing on our search for the -"

"Let's talk in private," John said firmly, cutting her off.

He turned to Cassie.

"I need you to find out how people are thinking," he continued. "Check the general feeling around town and report back to me. Toby's far from my favorite person, but there's a danger that more and more people are going to start listening to him. I don't know exactly what he's planning, but you can bet your bottom dollar it'll be just about the worst option possible."

As Cassie headed away across the street, John turned to Lisa.

"Sorry," he murmured, "but I didn't want you saying more about the search for the pendant, not in front of her."

"Do you think Cassie might be the Walker?" she asked.

"Not particularly," he explained, "but we need to be extremely cautious. If the wolves learn that we can't find it, that'll be the green light they've been waiting for. They've been cautious so far because they still aren't certain that it's missing. If they find out the truth, there's absolutely nothing stopping them storming into the town and doing whatever they want."

"So where are we going to look?" Lisa replied, as Eloise clung to her hand.

"We've tried all the obvious places," John admitted. "The church, the town hall, the station... even McGinty's."

"I checked Joe's haul in the garage," she told him. "I really thought there was a chance it might be there. I didn't like Joe Hicks one bit, but he knew this town inside out and if anyone might have known about the pendant, it would have been him." She paused for a few seconds. "Hey, do you have a minute? There's somewhere that might be able to give us a little inspiration."

***

"The town museum?" John said, following Lisa and Eloise into a room at the rear of the town hall. "You told me you checked in here already."

"I did," Lisa replied, "but I was looking for the pendant itself, when maybe I should have been looking for ideas instead."

"Come again?"

"I remember Dad laughing about this place when it was first set up, and making fun of it," she said as she looked at some old hats that had been put on display in a cabinet next to various mannequins. "He thought no-one in their right mind would ever want to see a load of old tat like this. To be honest, he might have had a point, but right now the museum is our best shot at getting an overview of the town's history."

She walked to another cabinet and saw some old books.

"The pendant is part of that history," she added, lost in thought for a moment. "Somewhere during that history, it got lost."

"I'm glad the uniform has changed a little," John said, stopping to look at a mannequin wearing the clothes of an old sheriff. "That thing looks itchy as hell."

Spotting some woodcut engravings nearby, he wandered over and saw a large image showing a man fighting a wolf. A shiver ran through his bones as he thought back to his night in the forest, and as he focused on the wolf he couldn't help but wonder exactly what he'd become.

"For a town that claims there are no wolves around," he continued, "the people of Sobolton sure spend a lot of time talking about the damn things."

"It was obviously a kind of collective denial of reality," she suggested, leading Eloise across the room so that they too could look at the engravings. "Perhaps it was a form of folk memory. People might not have known the details of the pendant, but they had some kind of shared belief that they were safe from the wolves. Over the years, they reinforced that belief by telling themselves the same stories over and over again."

She turned to John, and for a few seconds she caught a strange faraway expression in his eyes, along with some familiar quality that she couldn't quite put her finger on.

"Are you finding it hard to believe?" she added.

"Am I finding *what* hard to believe?"

"All this stuff about werewolves," she continued. "You're an outsider, you didn't grow up in Sobolton. As I understand it, you're a New York guy. Coming here and hearing all this stuff must hit you kind of different."

She waited for an answer, but there was still something about him that seemed a little odd. Although she couldn't be certain, she felt as if there was some small aspect of his expression that reminded her almost of Michael. At the same time, she told herself that the calm, quiet and stoic John Tench couldn't possibly have anything at all to do with the crazed maniac who'd kept her trapped in the cabin.

Suddenly John turned to her.

Before she could stop herself, Lisa instinctively took a step back.

"What?" John asked. "What is it? What's wrong?"

"Nothing," Lisa replied unconvincingly.

"Why are you looking at me like that?"

She glanced at the engravings again, trying to act normal, but her heart was racing and she immediately found herself looking at an image showing a man halfway through a transformation into his wolf form.

"I was just... thinking for a moment," she said finally. "About the Walker. It'd have to be someone who's been around for a while, right?"

"That seems to be the whole idea."

"Okay, good," she continued, telling herself that John couldn't possibly be the culprit. She watched the engravings for a moment longer, before turning to him again. "It's so hard when you realize that you basically have to suspect everyone. I mean, I know *I'm* not the Walker, and I know Eloise isn't as well, but literally anyone else in the entire town could be spying on us all for the wolves."

"We only have one clue so far," he told her. "If the Walker knew that we've lost the pendant, they'd have told the wolves by now and we'd probably be in the middle of their most ferocious attack yet."

"So who knows we can't find the pendant?"

"You and me," he continued, "and obviously Eloise." He thought for a moment. "Bob knows too."

"What about other people at the station?"

"A few people have been around us when we've talked about it, before I knew to keep my mouth shut," he admitted. "No-one else, though. Oh, apart from Father Rousseau at the church."

"So that makes five or six people at most," she pointed out. "We really haven't narrowed it down very much, have we?"

"No, we have not," he said with a heavy sigh. "The thing I don't understand is that this pendant was important. I'm sure that in every generation, people knew that it had to be protected, so why was it allowed to get lost like this? And even if that happened, shouldn't someone have tried to find it by now?"

"I've got a feeling Joe Hicks might have been onto that a while ago," she told him. "From looking at the stuff in his garage, I got the sense that he was definitely searching for something important. I hated the guy, I mean I really loathed him with every fiber of my being, but... I'm starting to think that in his own corrupt way, he was genuinely trying to keep the entire town safe."

"I agree," John admitted. "I think it's time to work out exactly what Joe knew."

CHAPTER SIX

Sobolton, USA – 1869...

"OVER THERE!" JIMMY GARRETT shouted, pointing to the right and immediately guiding his horse in that direction. "There's a fire!"

Along with the other men who'd ridden out from town, Patrick Cochrane forced his horse to follow. They picked their way over rough, rocky ground near the shore of the lake, and sure enough they soon came upon a small encampment with a smoldering fire that had been built in the middle of a circle of rocks. The encampment had clearly been abandoned, but not too long ago, and some animal bones had been left discarded on the ground.

"Filthy bastards," Jimmy said, still on his horse as he looked around for some hint of the bandits' location. "They took what they wanted and now they've already moved on."

"So where does that leave us?" Tom Buchanan asked. "This is exactly what happened six months ago. People said maybe they wouldn't come back again, but they sure did."

"We need to be better prepared for next time," Jimmy said darkly. "There's no point chasing after them now, we'd only be wasting our time. Hopefully they'll have some bad luck in one of the neighboring towns soon. I'm starting to think that's the only way we'll ever be rid of them."

"Are you sure it's the same bandits every time?" Patrick asked.

"We've seen the whites of their eyes," Jimmy told him. "We had a big old shootout with them once, but they still got away. It's the same two bastards, just a little older each year."

"Is that our strategy now?" Tom said. "Are we just gonna wait for them to drop dead of old age?"

"They probably went that way," Patrick added, nodding toward a trail that led into the forest. "Wouldn't that take them around the edge of the lake while giving them plenty of cover? They might not even have gone very far."

"We can't go hunting them," Jimmy replied, sounding irritated by the suggestion. "Not in there. They'd just ambush us."

"They took silver from the men they killed this morning," Tom pointed out. "They're probably too busy counting it all and laughing at us."

"We're heading back into town," Jimmy said, turning his horse around and starting to lead the others back the way they'd all just come. "There's no point in us all being out here like this. We've got other work to do."

"Are you just gonna give up and let them go?" Patrick asked, shocked by their attitude.

"There's nothing we can do about them now," Jimmy called back to him, "not if we're not quick enough to catch them in a spot like this. Once they're gone, they're gone. We just have to face the fact that they have an advantage in that regard. They'll slip up one day, though. We'll catch 'em napping or something like that, and then we'll make 'em pay. Until that happens, though, we've just gotta bide out time and be patient."

"There's such a thing as too much patience," Patrick replied, but the other men were all already too far away to hear him.

Left alone, still on the horse, Patrick looked down at the encampment. He knew the others were probably right, and that they had a much better idea of the local area, but at the same time he hated the idea that a pair of bandits could cause so much trouble not only to Sobolton but evidently to half a dozen other towns in the area. Taking a deep breath, he tried to muster the necessary acceptance, but a moment later he looked at the forest again. As far as he could tell, there was really only one likely route that the bandits might have taken, and he couldn't help thinking that the people of Sobolton were giving up too easily.

"This is probably a mistake," he said to the horse, before guiding it toward the trail that led into the forest. "Let's just take a quick look, and hope that it's not a fatal one."

***

A couple of hours later, having emerged from the forest at another section of the shore, Patrick was starting to feel that the others had been right after all. He'd seen no obvious sign that the bandits – or anyone else for that matter – might be around, and he knew that soon he'd have to turn back if he didn't want to risk getting stuck away from town in the dark.

The sun was already dipping in the sky, and the ripples on the lake's surface had lost their earlier brightness.

"Looks like we're on a hiding to nothing, Blackspot," he muttered. "That's your name, isn't it? I think -"

In that instant he heard a distinctive clicking sound that he knew could only one thing. His first thought was that he'd somehow wandered into a trap, and his second thought -

Suddenly a shot rang out, hitting him in the shoulder and sending him tumbling back off the horse, which immediately bolted and raced away. With his right foot caught momentarily in one of the stirrups, Patrick was slammed against an exposed tree root before coming loose, rolling away from the path once his foot was free.

Letting out a pained gasp, he came to a rest at the bottom of a narrow slope. He immediately rolled to one side and took shelter under an overhanging set of roots, and then – as his heart pounded and blood began to leak from the wound in his shoulder – he pulled his gun out and checked that it was loaded.

Somewhere nearby, footsteps scrambled across the rocks.

Swallowing hard, he listened carefully and quickly realized that he'd been ambushed by not one but two people. Assuming that these must be the same two bandits who'd been harassing Sobolton and other towns, he figured that they were clearly well-practiced and had decent aims, even if their first shot hadn't quite managed to finish him off.

He listened, and after a few more seconds he became aware of footsteps slowly edging closer to his left.

"You there!" a voice shouted from over his

shoulder, somewhere off to the right. "Sorry for that little misunderstanding. If you'd like to come out and show yourself, I'm sure we can straight it all out real fast."

Immediately realizing that they were trying to trap him in a classic pincer movement, he shifted to look over to his left.

"What's a bullet between friends?" the man in the other direction yelled, still clearly trying to distract him. "I'd sure like to apologize to you face to face. Man to man, like."

Convinced that the man with the voice was a fair distance away still, Patrick realized that the other man – somewhere nearby to his left – was going to do the shooting. He waited, watching for any hint of movement, and finally he spotted a shadow moving across the rocks.

Leaning out, Patrick fired twice, hitting the man in the chest and sending him slumping down.

More gunshots rang out nearby, and as he pulled back to take cover Patrick told himself that at least now the numbers were more even. He felt fairly sure that the first man was dead, and now he listened as someone raced toward the trees. In that moment he understand that the second man, rather than trying to take revenge for his comrade's death, was actually running away like a common coward.

Fully aware of the risk, Patrick got to his feet and turned just in time to see the man racing off into the forest. Despite the pain in his shoulder, he raised his gun and took a few seconds to aim, and then he fired twice. One of the shots hit the man in the back of the head, blowing part of his skull away and sending his lifeless corpse skittering down against one of the trees.

Turning to look all around, Patrick quickly determined that there were no other men nearby. He could see Blackspot lingering over by the shoreline, and he told himself that he'd be able to quickly get the horse back. Checking the wound on his own shoulder, he saw that the bullet seemed to have passed through cleanly enough and that it had burst out from the other side. He could still move his arm and the flow of blood – all things considered – wasn't nearly as bad as it could have been.

Still driven in part by adrenaline, he began to clamber over the rocks, heading over to Blackspot. As he did so, he realized that he needed to take some kind of trophy back to prove to the people of Sobolton that the bandits were dead. He didn't much fancy carting the two corpses over such a long distance, but as he stopped to look down at one of the bandits he realized that the man had been carrying a long serrated knife attached to his belt.

"Hold on, Blackspot," he muttered, not particularly enthused by the prospect of what he was going to have to do next. "Before we head home, I just need to do a spot of cutting."

AMY CROSS

CHAPTER SEVEN

Today...

"AND WHY IN THE name of all that's holy -"

Loretta Hicks took a moment to make the sign of the cross against her chest before continuing.

"- should I consent to let you do that?"

"It's a matter of the town's safety," John said, having just removed his hat as a mark of respect. "Mrs. Hicks, I understand that I'm not your favorite person right now but -"

"You've got that right!" she barked.

"We think there might be something in your husband's possessions that could help us," he explained. "Something that could save the whole town."

"She already looked in the garage," Loretta replied, nodding in Lisa's general direction.

"Mrs. Hicks," John continued, "your husband was a respected public servant for decades in this town. He worked tirelessly to keep the people of Sobolton safe, and we now have reason to believe that he can still help even -"

"Even from beyond the grave," Lisa interjected.

"Is that right?" Loretta muttered skeptically, before looking down at Eloise.

Eloise, in return, offered what she hoped would be taken as a sweet smile.

Loretta merely glared back at her.

"Joe and my dad were close," Lisa pointed out. "I got to know Joe – I hope you don't mind me calling him Joe – and I know that he would've really wanted us to explore every avenue here. If we're right, he started working on something vitally important, something that would have eventually made him a hero. You don't want all of that work to get wasted, do you?"

"There's no need to try buttering me up," Loretta told her sniffily, before pausing for a few seconds. In the background, the television could be heard blaring in the house, with voices arguing on some cable news show. "It's not locked. Get in there and take a look around, but don't go removing anything without my permission."

***

"I'm getting a severe case of deja vu," Lisa admitted a short while later, as she stood balancing on a child's stool and reached toward the top boxes at the back of the garage. "I searched in here before, John, and there was no sign of the pendant or anything else that might be useful."

"I'm not doubting you for one moment," he replied as he dug through another box on the garage's cracked concrete floor, with a couple of spiders quickly scurrying away. "I just feel like..."

He hesitated, looking at a bunch of slightly damp books about local history.

"I just feel," he continued cautiously, "like perhaps I misjudged Joe Hicks. And believe me, I feel slightly dirty even saying those words."

"Same."

She turned to him.

"Joe Hicks was instrumental in getting me sent to Lakehurst," she reminded him. "He was instrumental in a lot of bad things. Because of that, I guess I wrote him off as some kind of... almost cartoonish evil monster. Now, though, I'm starting to think that even if I personally suffered at his hands, I need to look at the broader picture of what he was trying to do. I need to look past my own feelings and think about what's best for the whole town."

"He was a complicated man," John murmured as he opened another box.

"What's Lakehurst?" Eloise asked.

"Nothing," Lisa said quickly, turning to see that her daughter was sitting obediently on an old chair nearby. "Nothing you need to worry about, at least."

"Joe and I might not have agreed on the methods," John continued, holding up a dusty and scratched glass vase, "but I'm pretty sure that we had a common goal in mind. In his own roundabout way, Joe was trying to save the town." He glanced at Lisa. "I don't condone how he went about things. Not for one second, because I know that innocent people got hurt and -"

"Save me the pity party," she replied, cutting him off. "Especially in front of... you know who."

John turned to see that Eloise was now examining an old coloring book.

"Let's focus on why we came here," he suggested, reaching into the box and pulling out a pair of old candlesticks. "We're not even sure that Joe discovered anything, and I can't help thinking that if he did, he would have been more -"

Suddenly he let out a gasp of pain. Pulling back, he dropped to his knees with the candlesticks still clasped in his hands. He winced, and now his hands were shaking wildly as cracks began to burn through his skin.

"John?" Lisa called out, jumping down from the stool and hurrying over to him. "What's wrong?"

"Mommy, what's happening to him?" Eloise asked.

"John, talk to me," Lisa continued, kneeling in front of him and seeing that blood was fizzing as it dribbled from his hands. "John, can you let go of those? Can you try?"

Gritting his teeth, John tried to focus on releasing his grip on the candlesticks, but for a moment that task seemed utterly impossible. Finally, however, he was able to slowly prise his fingers away, revealing his burned palms as the candlesticks fell harmlessly onto the floor.

"What happened?" Lisa asked, watching with horror as he turned his hands around. In a few patches, the flesh had burned away to expose tendons and even bone beneath.

Realizing that John was in too much pain to respond, she reached a hand toward the nearest candlestick. At first she didn't dare to touch it, but after a few seconds she gently brushed her knuckles against the surface; surprised to feel no pain at all, she checked the other candlestick, and a moment later she picked them both up.

"Were they live or something?" she gasped,

turning to see that the flesh of John's palms was still sizzling slightly. "I don't understand. What -"

Before she could finish, an idea popped into the back of her mind. She turned the candlesticks around, and although she was no expert, something about their slightly tarnished appearance made her wonder whether they might in fact be quite old, perhaps even...

"Silver," she whispered.

"I'm okay," John gasped, leaning back against the wall as he struggled to get his breath back. "I'm fine."

"But..."

She looked at his hands, then at the candlesticks again, and finally she let them go as she slowly got to her feet and began to back away.

"I'm okay," John said again, more firmly this time. "I don't know what happened, but it's just a little burn. I'll be fine in a minute or two, just give me a chance."

"The silver did that to you," she replied, taking another step back and instinctively reaching a hand out toward Eloise, encouraging her to move closer. "The silver burned your hands. I've only ever seen that happen to one person before, and that was..."

"Lisa, it's not what you're thinking," John said, swallowing hard as he tried to get to his feet, only to find that he was still a little too weak. "Can you please just hold on for a moment? I'll explain everything and -"

"It's you," she said firmly.

"What are you -"

"You're the Walker."

"Of course I'm not!" he hissed angrily. "Are you insane?"

"The Walker is a werewolf who mingles with the people of Sobolton," she continued. "You kept saying over and over again that it had to be someone who'd been here for a long time, but what if that wasn't true? What if the previous Walker left or died or something, and they needed a new one? You've been here for less than a year, right?"

"Lisa -"

"And if you're not the Walker," she added, "then why did those silver candlesticks burn your hands like that?"

He opened his mouth to reply, but at the last second he held back as he realized that he wasn't quite sure how to explain everything. He wanted to tell her that it was all fine, that there was no reason to worry; the last thing he needed to do was admit to his recent blackouts or to his experience waking up naked in the forest, but he could see the fear in her eyes now and he was starting to realize that he could hide the truth no longer.

"Lisa," he said finally, already feeling a little stronger, "I want you to listen to me very carefully. I'm not the Walker. Far from it. In fact, I -"

"Run!" she shouted, suddenly grabbing Eloise's hand and pulling her out of the garage. "We have to get out of here!"

"Lisa, wait!" John yelled, this time hauling himself up, still clutching his hands as he began to shuffle after her. "You've got it all wrong! Lisa, come back so I can explain!"

CHAPTER EIGHT

Sobolton, USA – 1869...

A SEVERED HUMAN HEAD, which had once belonged to one of the bandits, fell with a dull thud onto the ground, followed a moment later by the second.

The eyes of the two dead men stared up in frozen horror toward the early evening sky.

"Well," Ignacious said, clearly lost for words as he stared at the gruesome sight, "that's surely them, alright. We all got glimpses of them in the past. These are the two fellows who've been messing not only with us, but with most of the towns for miles around. Looks like..."

Leaning down, he peered more closely at the two heads, which had been crudely cut away from their necks. One of the head was more badly damaged than the other, yet Ignacious was in no doubt that there were indeed the men who'd caused so much trouble. After a moment he stood up straight, wincing as he felt a pain in the small of his back, and then he turned to see Patrick Cochrane standing nearby.

"You're hurt," he pointed out.

"I need stitching up," Patrick replied, ignoring the patch of blood on his own shoulder. "And cleaning. But I'll be fine."

"You've been here less than a day," Ignacious continued. "You haven't even spent the night, and already you've fixed up the biggest problem we here in Sobolton were facing."

"Anyone would have one the same."

"Sure, but anyone *didn't*," Ignacious pointed out, before turning to the gathered crowd. "Is Sarah Higgins or Mrs. Lobotham here?" he called out. "This man's in need of some medical attention! Can someone fetch somebody who knows how to help him?"

A murmur spread across the crowd, and after just a few seconds Sarah Higgins squeezed through and made her way over to Patrick.

"And when you're done with that," Ignacious continued, "I'd like a word with you in private, Mr. Cochrane. I think you and I have a number of matters we need to discuss."

***

"Was there a bounty on their heads?" Walter Wade asked breathlessly as he hurried ahead of Patrick, entering the office and making his way over to the main desk. "Was there? How much was it worth?"

"There was no bounty," Ignacious replied. "In truth, we didn't think it'd do much good. That, and we couldn't really afford any bounty that'd bring us much help."

He watched as Patrick, with his shoulder now bandaged, made his way through the open doorway.

"At least," he added, "that's what we told ourselves."

"I don't want any fuss," Patrick said, and his boots thumped hard against the wooden floor as he crossed the room and finally joined Walter in front of the desk. "Like I told you out there, anyone would've done the same. Those two men weren't really up to much, not if they could be so easily taken down like that. They were a pair of opportunists, that's all. I'm glad to rid the world of their kind whenever I get the chance."

"I like your attitude," Ignacious told him, unable to stifle a faint smile as he slipped his hands into a pair of gloves. "I like it a very great deal."

"I don't mean to be rude," Patrick replied,

"but I'd sure like to get back out there and find myself somewhere to sleep for the night."

"Oh, don't worry about that," Ignacious replied. "Somewhere to sleep is the least of your concerns right now. At least, assuming you're interested in my offer."

"Offer?" Walter asked excitedly, looking constantly from one man to the other. "What offer?"

"That's a good question," Patrick murmured. "What offer?"

Ignacious opened a drawer in the desk. He fumbled for a moment through the contents, before pulling out a slightly dented metal badge with six points.

"What's that for?" Walter asked, reaching out to grab the badge. "What -"

"Paws off!" Ignacious said firmly, pushing his hand away before holding the badge up so that Patrick could see it better. "Son, do you know what this is?"

Peering at the badge, John saw that it appeared to a badge made for a sheriff. Sure, it was a little rough around the edges, but he'd seen similar badges before. The only difference was that this particular badge had a small bump in its center, as if something had been set into the metal.

"Who's the sheriff around here?" he asked cautiously.

"We don't have one," Ignacious explained.

"We have a mayor – that's me – and a blacksmith, and a priest, and a few other people in important roles. We're still filling out our ranks, so to speak. We don't have a doctor, which is a big problem, and we also don't have..."

His voice trailed off, and then he slowly limped around the desk until he was standing in front of Patrick.

"We've not had a sheriff yet," he continued. "We've sort of muddled along for ourselves. A few people have made remarks about needing someone, but nobody could agree on who. As the mayor, I've tried to force the issue, albeit without a great deal of luck so far. However, given that today you accomplished something that none of the rest of the boys in town could manage, I don't think there'd be much argument if I were to award the position to you."

"You want *me* to become your sheriff?"

"The first sheriff of Sobolton," Ignacious continued, and now his eyes were bright with anticipation. "The role would come with accommodation, naturally, and you'd be paid as well. I'm not promising that it'd be easy, but you'd have the respect of everyone here and I truly believe that you'd be able to get a lot done. We don't have a jail, not yet, but I can put some men to work on that immediately."

He held the badge out.

"If you'd consider staying and taking on this title," he added, "we'd all be extraordinarily grateful." He leaned closer and lowered his voice. "This wouldn't be an official part of the compensation package," he added, "but I would be most happy to arrange a bride for you as well. We have several lovely young ladies of the right age. Marion Doggett's pretty, if you don't mind bad teeth, or Susan Harker's more of a decent all-rounder."

"The accommodation and wage would be more than sufficient," Patrick replied.

"Are you sure?"

"I'm sure. I'll find my own wife, when the right moment comes."

"I guess that's up to you," Ignacious told him, before holding the badge up a little higher. "To be frank, Mr. Cochrane, we need a man like you here in Sobolton. This town is growing, and I see great potential for its future, which is why I've been at such pains to get us organized. If you'll take up this offer, that means I really only need to find a doctor and then we'll all be pointing in the right direction, so to speak. I don't know if you were particularly planning on hanging around, but it seems to me that this opportunity could serve us both extremely well."

Patrick hesitated, staring at the badge as if he really wasn't sure.

"Let's see how it looks on you," Ignacious added, taking a moment to pin the badge onto Patrick's lapel. He carefully turned it a little, then he brushed the lapel clean, and finally he stepped back and admired his work. "Why, it suits you down to the ground!" he exclaimed. "I wish I had a mirror so you could see for yourself!"

He turned to Wade.

"You there," he continued, "I forget your name, but doesn't he look swell with that badge on his chest? Tell him he looks the part!"

"Are you in need of a deputy?" Walter asked.

"I didn't mean to stay here for too long," Patrick admitted, looking down at the badge on his chest, "and I sure never considered myself to be a candidate for a role as a lawman." He paused, giving the matter a little more consideration. "But I'm a civic-minded man," he continued cautiously, "and I like to help where I can. I'd be happy to take up your kind offer, Mr. Huddlestone, and I promise that I'll do my utmost to keep the town safe. I already saw that you have a saloon, so I imagine you also have a problem with drunkenness. I should warn you, though, that I don't take kindly to bad behavior. I'll be fair but firm."

"That's exactly what we want," Ignacious replied, clearly massively relieved as he headed to the door. "Come on, let's get out there and I'll give everyone the good news."

"Is that offer of finding a wife still open?" Walter asked as he followed the other two men out of the office. "As the official deputy, I sure could use someone to keep me warm at night!"

CHAPTER NINE

Today...

"IT'S OKAY," LISA SAID, holding Eloise's hand tight as she led her daughter along the street. "There's no need to be scared. We're just going to find somewhere to... sit for a while."

"Why are you upset?" Eloise asked.

"I'm not."

As those words left her lips, and as she looked around for some spot where she might be able to stop and come up with a plan, Lisa realized that she sounded absolutely terrified. Her heart was pounding and her mind was racing, and all she really knew was that she had to get as far away from Sheriff John Tench as possible. She'd seen the proof that he was a wolf in human form, and she figured that could only mean that he was the insidious Walker in the heart of the town.

Now she had to work out who she could *really* trust.

She was in the Eden Hills part of Sobolton, slightly away from the center. She knew this part well from her childhood days, but a lot had changed in the twenty years she'd spent trapped in Michael's cabin. As she turned and looked in every direction, she saw that the old gas station was still open and that the church was still standing; a lot of the stores had changed, however, and she was starting to realize just how few people she still knew. She had no cellphone with her and no way of contacting anyone, and for a few more seconds she felt completely alone.

"Is it because he's a wolf?" Eloise asked.

Lisa turned and looked down at her.

"Is that why you're scared?" the little girl continued.

"How did you know?" she replied.

"Isn't it obvious?" Eloise suggested. "I thought *you* already knew. It's really easy to tell."

"We don't have time to talk about this right now," Lisa said, leading her away from the intersection, picking a street that she knew would eventually lead them back into the center of town. She knew she had to avoid John, but at the same time she also knew she had to find someone who could help, and in that moment there was only one person she could think of.

"We're going to find Doctor Law," she explained as they made their way over the crosswalk. "We'll -"

Stopping as soon as they reached the other side, she realized that running to Robert Law would be far too obvious. She looked along the street, and in that moment she remembered that – many years earlier – there had been one person who'd lived just a couple of blocks away, someone she'd always trusted implicitly. She considered the possibility for a moment, and then she began to lead Eloise along a different street while telling herself that hopefully John would have no idea where she was going next.

"Where are you taking me?" Eloise asked. "Doctor Law doesn't live down here, does he?"

"No," she replied, quickly spotting a familiar house up ahead, "but someone else does."

***

"Of course it's alright," Rachel said, opening her front door more fully as Lisa and Eloise stepped into the house. "I was going to see if you wanted to meet up for a coffee soon, anyway, and -"

"We need to hide out here for a little while," Lisa replied, turning to her while trying to not seem too crazy. "Do you know how to get in touch with

Robert Law?"

"The doctor?" Rachel thought for a moment. "I think -"

"Shut the door!"

After pushing the door shut, Rachel headed into the front room.

"I don't really know the guy," she explained, grabbing her cellphone and unlocking the screen, then bringing up a number and getting ready to call, "but I'll ask at the sheriff's station and -"

"No!" Lisa gasped, hurrying over and pulling the phone from her hands.

"What's wrong?" Rachel replied. "Lisa, I've never seen you like this before."

"We can't involve anyone at the station," Lisa insisted. "The station has been compromised."

"Compromised? How?"

"Sheriff Tench..."

Her voice trailed off for a moment. She knew full well that she probably seemed to be utterly out of her mind, yet she figured she could hardly backtrack and claim everything was fine now. Glancing at Eloise, she saw the fear in her daughter's eyes and told herself that she had to pull herself together.

"We just can't risk going through Sheriff Tench's office," she told Rachel finally. "It's a long and complicated story, but for now you just have to take my word for it. Sheriff Tench is..."

Rachel waited.

"He's..."

After a moment, Rachel tilted her head slightly.

"Sheriff Tench is a werewolf," Lisa said finally. "If you don't believe me, ask Eloise, apparently she sensed it a while ago. The point is, Tench is the Walker, which is a werewolf that lives in our town and keeps its ear to the ground. If anything relevant happens in Sobolton at all, the Walker relates it to the wolves in the forest. If you think about it, having a wolf become the sheriff was a genius move on their part. He's right in the middle of things and he knows pretty much everything that goes on in the town. They probably heard that Joe Hicks was on his way out and engineered Tench as his replacement."

"Okay," Rachel said cautiously, "but... why?"

"They need to know whether we can defend ourselves," Lisa explained. "There's this pendant that can supposedly defeat the wolves, it's been in the town for centuries but now it's lost. If the wolves find out that we can't locate that pendant, they'll realize that the whole town is vulnerable. They'll come in force, and they'll take -"

Stopping herself just in time, she looked over to see that Eloise was listening keenly to every word that left her mouth.

"They'll take whatever they want," Lisa continued, choosing her words more carefully now as she turned to Rachel again. "I think you understand what I'm getting at, Rachel. Tench knows that we can't find the pendant, he's obviously been helping search for it because he wants to snatch it away from us. Sobolton has long lived in fear of the wolves, even if people refused to admit that fact. This is a conflict that goes back centuries, and without the pendant we don't have any hope."

"How can one stupid pendant have so much power?" Rachel asked.

"I don't have a clue," Lisa admitted. "I only just realized that Tench is the Walker. The good news is that there should only be one of them at any given time, so that means we can trust everyone else."

"We should be grateful for small mercies, I guess," Rachel muttered. "So this pendant... is it truly gone? You've checked everywhere and you can't find it?"

"I still think it's somewhere in the town," Lisa told her, "but that doesn't help us very much. We don't even know how or why it got lost. Someone probably has it without even realizing that it's so important, but we can't advertise that fact too widely because then John might get his hands on it first. Then again, I don't know whether he actually needs to find it, or whether it's just enough for him to know that we don't have it. And even if it turns up, I have no idea exactly how powerful it is."

"Well," Rachel replied, "we all certainly seem to be in a pickle, then, don't we?"

"There's a way to fix this," Lisa continued, sitting on the edge of the sofa with Eloise still right next to her. "There has to be. We can't just let them win. We have to fight back and -"

Before she could finish, they all heard a loud knock on the front door.

"Lisa?" John called out from the other side. "It's John Tench. I know you're in there and I'd really like to talk to you."

"How did he find us?" she whispered.

"Do you want to go out the back?" Rachel asked. "There's a way out into an alley, and you could try to run."

"He'd just keep tracking us down," Lisa replied, watching the door as she tried to work out how she could get away. "He knows everything, he knows we're defenseless, and now he's come to take everything from us." With tears in her eyes, she turned to Eloise. "But I won't let him. I can't. There has to be a way to stop him, to make him see reason. There has to be some way to get through to him."

"Lisa," John said, knocking on the door again, "I know this is difficult, but I can explain. Lisa, please... will you at least listen to me?"

CHAPTER TEN

Sobolton, USA – 1869...

A WOMAN'S VOICE RANG out from the edge of the campfire as she sang tales about Sobolton's past. Her voice carried far through the small town, and a fair crowd had turned out to listen now that darkness had fallen.

Standing on the porch outside McGinty's, the local saloon, Patrick let the woman's song wash over him. He'd been in the town for less that twenty-four hours and now he was facing his first night; already he was starting to feel strangely at home, and he couldn't help but wonder whether a curious combination of fate and circumstances might have delivered him to a place where he might actually make a difference. After wandering for so long since he'd stopped fighting, for the first time he found himself not actively contemplating hitting the road again.

Yet as the woman continued to sing, occasionally he heard echoes of gunfire in his mind, as if some deep part of his soul insisted on constantly remembering the worst moments from the battlefield.

"Evening, Sheriff Cochrane," a voice said, and Patrick turned to see that two men had wandered over to join him.

He opened his mouth to ask how they even knew who he was, but a moment later he looked down and saw the badge pinned to his shirt. He knew, also, that word probably traveled fast in a small community like Sobolton.

"Clay Lacy," the first man said, stepping forward and reaching out to shake his hand.

"Randall Pierce," the second man added.

"We're sure glad to have you here," Clay continued. "We've been pushing Ignacious to get a sheriff in place for a while now, but he kept dragging his feet 'cause he said there was no-one suitable. Now you've turned up and you've already made Sobolton a safer place."

"I'm just trying my best," Patrick replied, feeling a little uncomfortable. Having never been a man who courted attention, he was starting to realize that he was now a pretty popular figure in the town. He paused, listening to the song for a moment. "Who's Nathaniel Wood?" he asked finally. "And... Temezin? Is that the name?"

"You've been listening to some of those old-time pieces, have you?" Clay chuckled, turning and looking over toward the campfire as the woman continued to sing. "It's not quite my kind of thing, personally."

"Is she singing about real people?"

"That depends on who you ask," Clay explained, turning to him. "Nathaniel Wood's supposedly some guy who showed up here and caused trouble, and Thomizen – I think that's how her name's pronounced, anyway – was apparently some woman who lived here in the early days of the town. There are plenty of different versions of their stories, you won't hear the exact same tale twice if you ask around. To be honest, if they were real, they lived a hundred years back or more and I can't quite bring myself to care too much."

"No-one even knows how Sobolton got its name," Randall added with a shrug. "I guess stuff like that just gets forgotten over time."

"All that wolf stuff's just a fairy tale for kids, anyway," Clay added. "I can't believe people even pretend to believe it."

"What wolf stuff?" Patrick asked.

"Forget about it," Clay told him, shaking his head. "You won't get far if you listen to some of the nonsense people spout round these parts, Sheriff Cochrane. If you ask me, we need to focus on the real threats in the area, not on a bunch of half-remembered crap in old songs that no-one even cares about anymore."

***

Making his way up the wooden steps leading into the small house that had been provided for him, Patrick was so lost in thought that for a moment he didn't even notice that the front door was open. Reaching out for the handle, he suddenly lost his train of thought and looked inside to see a dark-haired woman placing some sheets on the bed.

"Excuse me?" he said cautiously.

"Sheriff Cochrane!" the woman gasped, turning to him. "I'm sorry, I didn't know you'd be back so early. I thought you'd be with the others until later."

"Have we met?" he asked.

"Emma," she replied, stepping over to him and holding out a hand. "Emma McShane. Ignacious Huddlestone asked me to bring some things over to make this place a little more comfortable for you. I was just making up the bed and then I was going to find some bread and a few other items so that you'd have something to eat if you're hungry."

"That's very kind of you," he told her. "I don't need to be treated like I'm special, though. I can make my own bed and find my own meals."

"I think Mr. Huddlestone just wants to make a good impression," she explained. "To be honest, I think he's still worried that you might change your mind and... up and leave."

"Why would I do that?"

"I don't know. Perhaps because we're just a small town and you want to move on to bigger and better things?"

"I've had enough of moving on for a while," he told her. "I promised Mr. Huddlestone that I'd stick around. I had no idea that he was doubting my word on that matter."

"I'm sorry to have disturbed you," she replied, blushing slightly as she stepped past him. "I'll leave you alone. You're probably very tired and I'm sure you'll be wanting to get some rest."

"Can I ask you a question?"

Reaching the top of the steps outside, she stopped and turned to him.

"People in this town seem so worried about threats from outside," he continued, "but aside from those two bandits whose careers ended abruptly this afternoon, I'm not quite sure what's making everyone so... jumpy."

"I think it's just a hangover from the old days," she told him.

"What happened in the old days?"

"Well, some people -"

She held back for a moment, clearly worried about saying too much. Glancing over her shoulder, as if to make sure that she couldn't be overheard, she seemed to be on the verge of admitting something. Finally she stepped back into the room, approaching Patrick cautiously.

"My family's been here long enough," she continued, "that I've heard tales passed down from my grandfather, and from *his* grandfather before him."

"Tales about what, exactly?"

"Just superstitious things, really," she said, although the fear in her voice suggested that she wasn't convinced. "Sobolton's a growing town, but the more we spread the more we have to make inroads into the forest. There are lots of people here who work chopping down the trees so that we have space to build, and wood to use. And there are a few people who worry that the more we push into the forest, and the more we make changes to the local area, the more we risk... upsetting something."

"What exactly might there be out there to *get* upset?" he asked.

"Probably nothing," she admitted, "but that doesn't stop certain people worrying. But you can't hold back change, that much is certain. The Ringborn railroad's going to be coming through soon, and that's gonna bring a lot more people. If you ask me, years from now Sobolton's gonna be almost unrecognizable. It's even changed so much just in my lifetime. I also know that Ignacious has had some contact with people who want to send loggers down to really clear away much more of the forest. That'll happen not long from now, I'm sure."

"Sounds like this town might get rich," he suggested. "How can that be a bad thing?"

"I suppose it depends on what gets lost in the process," she told him, "and what gets disturbed too. I just worry that if we keep pushing into the forest, then eventually something might push back. I know I must sound foolish and I can't even put my finger on what might be out there. I just have this feeling inside whenever I look at the forest, and it's as if something's looking back at me. Sometimes I even think that the whole town is being watched."

"By what?"

"I'm sure I wouldn't know," she admitted. "And I hope very much that I'm wrong. I want nothing more than to see our town prosper. Please, you must ignore me when I witter on like his. Father always says that I -"

"Emma!" a voice called out in the distance. "Emma, where are you?"

"And that's him now," she said, taking a step back. "I should go to him. He's not been well since Mama died, and he often needs help. If you require anything more, just come and find me in the morning or ask Mr. Huddlestone. We're all just so glad to have you here, Sheriff Cochrane. You've already made such a big difference."

"I'm glad to be here too," he murmured, leaning against the doorway and watching as she hurried away into the darkness.

A moment later he looked beyond the town, and he saw the vast pitch-black forest spreading out under the starry night sky. For a few seconds he couldn't help but think about Emma's words, and he had to admit that he sure felt like something in the forest might well be watching the whole town.

CHAPTER ELEVEN

Today...

AS SOON AS THE front door creaked open and she saw John standing on the porch, Lisa felt an instinctual urge to run. She fought that urge, however, and she forced herself to step outside before turning to see Rachel and Eloise watching her the sofa.

"I won't be long," she told them both. "Remember what I told you to do if..."

Her voice trailed off, and then she shut the door before turning to John.

"You won't get her," she said firmly, although her voice didn't sound quite as defiant as she'd hoped. "I won't let you take her."

"I don't want to take her," he replied. "Lisa,

I'm on your side."

"Forgive me if I don't believe you."

"I'm not the Walker."

"I saw how the silver messed your with your skin."

He held up his hands, showing her that the palms – although mostly healed already – were still slightly mottled.

"What's that supposed to prove?" she asked.

"I guess I should have known that I couldn't hide it for long," he admitted. "Especially not from you, of all people." He took a deep breath, and then he let out a heavy sigh. "I'm not the Walker, but that doesn't mean that I'm not..."

She waited for him to continue, but she could tell that he was having trouble getting the words out.

"I can't say it," he admitted finally.

"What can't you say?" she asked.

"That word. To describe myself, I mean." He took another pause. "It happened on the night I tried to arrest Michael. I ended up with a bite on my hand, and since then, nothing has seemed quite right. I blacked out the other night and woke up in the forest without my clothes. When I got back into town, people were talking about a wolf that had intervened and -"

"That was you?"

"I don't know," he replied through gritted

teeth, "but I also have these flashes of memories that lead me to believe..."

Again, he seemed utterly lost.

"You've been turned," she said finally. "It's rare, I was under the impression that they don't like to do it, but if it's happened then... you've become one of them."

"I still can't be completely sure," he pointed out, "but the incident with the silver just now kind of seems to confirm it a little more. Believe me, I'm finding it very difficult to believe all of this and part of me still thinks that there's got to be some other explanation. I haven't told anyone else, because I'm still figuring it out myself. I don't know what triggers the transformation, if there's a transformation at all, and I don't know how much control I have over my actions when I'm in that... form."

They stood in silence for moment, each of them unsure as to what they should say next.

"You're taking it better than most people would," she said after a few more seconds.

"Does it really seem that way?" he asked. "Because right now, I'm freaking out."

"You're not showing it."

"My ex-wife always said I had a problem showing my emotions," he added with a faint smile. "I guess she had a point. I'm trying to hold it all in, when there's a genuine chance that I've become some kind of -"

Yet again, he stopped himself saying the word.

"Werewolf," she suggested. "You need to accept that fact. You're a werewolf now, John, like the wolves in the forest. Well, not exactly like them, because you're coming at it from the other side. They're wolves that can become human, and you're a human that can become a wolf."

"Is there a difference?"

"To them, yes, a massive difference. I know from hearing Michael talk that the natural born wolves tend not to trust humans who've been turned. In some cases they actively hate them."

"Well that's good news, then," he muttered, rolling his eyes. "Seems like I'm just not going to fit in anywhere, huh?"

***

A few minutes later, once she'd tentatively agreed to let John into the house, Lisa watched as he sat on a wooden chair facing Eloise. The girl, in turn, stepped toward him and reached a hand out, almost touching one side of his face before holding back at the last second.

"What is it?" John asked cautiously. "Can you sense it somehow?"

She paused, staring into his eyes, before

nodding.

"How?" he continued. "What is it about me that gives it away?"

"I don't know," she said softly.

"Do I *look* different?"

She thought about that for a moment, before shaking her head.

"Do -"

"It's your blood," she said suddenly.

"My blood?"

"It's stronger," she continued. "It's like mine, and not like..."

She turned to look over at her mother.

"It's okay, Eloise," Lisa said. "You don't have to be afraid."

"It's like mine," Eloise continued, turning to John again. "Don't you feel it when the moon's out? When the moon's strong, I feel it pulling on me. At the moment there's nothing, but if the moon's strong enough later, I'll feel like I'm having to try really hard to stop it happening."

"To stop *what* happening?" he replied.

She glanced at Lisa again, before leaning closer to John's ear.

"Turning into a wolf," she whispered.

"What did she say?" Lisa asked.

"This is nuts," Rachel added under her breath, having watched so far in absolute silence. "This is totally nuts. I feel like I'm tripping."

"Eloise," John said cautiously, "if you can sense this when you're near me, do you think that you could possibly sense it in someone else too?"

She thought about that question for a moment, and then she nodded again.

"How close would you have to be?" he continued.

"I don't know," she replied. "It's not all the time. Sometimes even with you, I barely notice it. Other times, like now, it's much stronger."

"But you *might* be able to sense it."

She nodded.

"How does this help?" Rachel asked.

"She might be able to identify the Walker," Lisa explained. "It's not a surefire thing, but right now it's just about the only chance we've got."

"Aren't you supposed to be looking for some kind of pendant?"

"That too," Lisa admitted. "But if the pendant is dangerous to the wolves, I'm starting to wonder whether there's some way that one of them might be able to help find it. John, do you think that's possible? Do you think that either you or Eloise might be able to sense the pendant if you get close?"

"Beats me," he admitted. "Eloise, what do you think?"

"I don't know," she said softly. "I want to help, but I don't really know what's happening." She paused again. "I know I've got a wolf in me," she added. "I can feel it sometimes. It's really strong and powerful, and it wants to come out, but I've never let it."

"You can keep it in?" he asked.

She nodded.

"I'd sure like to know how to do that," he told her. "I feel much less in control, like... it could burst out of me at any moment. I don't even know what could trigger it. Anger, or fear, or..."

"It's okay," she replied, "you'll get better at it. I was born like this, but I can tell that you're new to it. I can try to help you."

"I'd sure appreciate that," he said with a faint smile. "You know, for such a young lady, you seem to know an awful lot about certain things. I'm just sorry that you're in the middle of all this. You shouldn't be having to deal with monsters when you're a kid. We're the adults, *we* should be the ones dealing with all that stuff."

"I don't know what you mean," Eloise said cautiously. "Isn't it the same for everyone?"

"We should get moving," Lisa said suddenly, sniffing back tears as she got to her feet. "We still have two big problems on our hands, and those problems aren't going away soon. I don't know about you guys, but I really don't think that anyone would just lose the pendant, which means it's almost certainly hidden away somewhere in

Sobolton. Joe Hicks obviously couldn't find it, and I think we can assume that he searched high and low. So we need to think *not* like Joe for a moment."

"Can I help?" Rachel asked.

"Sorry," Lisa replied, "but I don't think so. We just need to keep searching and make sure that we don't attract the Walker's attention. Whoever he or she is, they probably know that we're up to something. If they figure out that we're still trying to find the pendant, that could be the signal for the wolves to launch an all-out war on the town."

She looked at Eloise for a moment and tried not to think about what might happen if Saint Thomas and his wolves got their hands on her.

"We don't have long," she added. "I'm worried about what might happen when the sun goes down tonight."

CHAPTER TWELVE

Sobolton, USA – 1869...

"SO I DON'T EXACTLY know what a deputy's supposed to do," Walter continued as he and Patrick sat on stools outside the makeshift sheriff's office the following morning, "but I suppose I just need to be ready in case I'm called upon to do... well, anything."

"That would be a good idea," Patrick said, distracted as he saw Emma McShane emerging from a nearby house and making her way along the dirty, dusty street. "You should..."

His voice trailed off, and in truth he wasn't much bothered about anything Walter said in that moment. Instead he found himself unable to stop watching Emma, and a moment later – as if she'd sensed his gaze on some deep level – she glanced in his direction and offered a smile.

Reaching up, he tipped his hat to her, and then he watched as she started talking to another woman.

"There are some fine specimens of ladyhood about, huh?" Walter said with a leering grin. "I don't know about you, Patrick, but I need to get myself a wife fast. The single life's no good for me. I want a woman who can do all the work at home while I'm out keeping the town safe. A strong man needs an obliging wife behind him. And under him."

"You're a deputy," Patrick pointed out, turning to him. "I would've thought that the ladies would be lining up to flutter their eyelashes at you."

"Perhaps word hasn't spread too far yet," Walter said, with a hint of disappointment in his voice as he scratched a spot behind his ear. "But how long do you think it'll take? I'm starting to think I might need to go and visit one of the ladies working upstairs at McGinty's."

"You mean the ladies I'm not supposed to know about?" Patrick asked with a slight smile. "I know what human nature's like. Some of these things just have to be tolerated, at least so long as they don't cause wider problems."

"So you wouldn't think less of me if I paid them a little visit later?" Walter asked.

"My opinion of you wouldn't change one

bit," Patrick said tactfully. "Just don't do it during working hours, alright? And don't get -"

Before he could finish, they both heard a woman screaming in the distance. Getting to his feet, Patrick hurried out into the middle of the street while automatically reaching for his gun, while Walter followed a few paces behind.

"Sheriff!" a man yelled at the far corner, waving at him frantically. "Get over here! Sal Weston's been attacked!"

***

"He lost too much blood," Sarah Higgins said after a moment's silence, before getting to her feet and taking a step back. "I'm sorry, but I couldn't do anything for him."

On the ground, the body of Sal Weston lay battered and bloodied, with thick cuts all over one side of his torso. The ferocious attack had extended to his head, too, with most of his right cheek having been torn away; a series of thick puncture wounds could be made out in his thin hair, glistening with yet more blood.

"We went out hunting," Paul May explained, "and we split up a little to see if we could get a jump on anything Suddenly I heard him crying out, and when I went back to him..."

He paused for a moment, before turning to

look around at the gathered crowd.

"It was a wolf," he continued, causing an immediate burst of excited chatter to spread in every direction. "I saw it as clear as I see any of you here now. It was a huge slathering wolf and it was damn near halfway to eating him. Sal'd be in its belly by now if I hadn't chased the damn thing off by throwing rocks at it!"

"Let's all calm down," Ignacious said, still out of breath after hurrying over from his office. "No-one's seen a wolf in these parts for as long as I've been alive and -"

"I'm not a liar!" Paul snapped angrily, turning to him. "I'm sorry, I'll stand for most things but I refuse to be called a liar!"

"No-one's calling you a liar," Ignacious replied, "but don't you think it's possible that you might have been... mistaken?"

"I know what a wolf looks like," Paul told him. "Before I came to Sobolton I saw plenty of 'em."

"I just don't see why a wolf would suddenly come to the area and attack a man like this," Ignacious continued. "It doesn't make any sense, is what I'm saying. Why would a wolf show up and suddenly get a taste for blood like this? What kind of... what..."

As his voice trailed off, he removed his hat and wiped sweat from his brow. The small crowd, meanwhile, had also fallen silent, as if nobody was quite prepared yet to give voice to some kind of shared fear. People were glancing uncertainly at one another, and slowly a series of whispers began to break out. Ignacious, meanwhile, took a seat on a nearby bench and still seemed to be struggling with the heat. Leaning on his cane, he looked over at Sal's corpse as if he was hoping that it might suddenly disappear and be revealed as nothing more than a feverish nightmare.

"They're back," a voice said suddenly.

Silence returned.

"We all know it," Randall Pierce said from his spot in the crowd. "We're all thinking it. Why's no-one else saying it?"

"We don't know anything of the sort," Clay Lacy cautioned him.

"We know wolves have plagued this town in the past," Randall continued, and now there was a hint of desperation in his voice. "We know that by the grace of God, they've left us alone for a while. But what if they're back now and this is just a warning shot?"

"You've never been superstitious before," Clay replied. "Why -"

"It's not superstition if it's true!" Randall snapped, turning to him.

"He's right," a woman nearby murmured, before making the sign of the cross against her chest. "The Lord has seen fit to remove his protection from us and now we're to be devoured by these things."

"No-one's getting devoured by anything," Clay said with a sigh.

"Apart from poor Sal," Randall reminded him. "So far."

"That wolf was angry and hungry," Paul May added. "But it wasn't starving."

The others looked over at him.

"I've seen 'em when they're starving," he continued. "They have this kind of ferocity about 'em that's born out of necessity. They need to feed to survive, like all animals. To be honest, I can almost bring myself to respect that. But this one today was different. It was big and strong, and it looked like it had been fed well for a long time. So it didn't attack out of hunger, like all wolf attacks I've seen before. This one was attacking because..."

He paused as he tried to think of the right word.

"It was a warning," Randall suggested.

"Seemed that way to me," Paul replied quickly. "Seemed like the wolf was mighty comfortable, like he thought we'd wandered into his territory so we were fair game, but we weren't far out of town."

"If there's one, there'll be more," Randall said, bringing a murmur of agreement from the gathered townsfolk.

"You don't know that," Clay told them. "None of you do. It might be just passing through."

"Or it's the first of many," Randall continued, "in which case, we need to send a warning of our own. We need to get out there and hunt that thing down so that we give them all a message. Then we need to hang its pelt up so all the other wolves understand to keep away."

"Are we going hunting?" Walter Wade asked excitedly. "I've never eaten wolf meat before, but I'm sure willing to give it a try. Hell, we can have ourselves a goddamn victory feast!"

"Let's all calm down a little," Ignacious said, finally getting to his feet again while still wiping some sweat from his face. "No good'll come of anyone rushing out into the forest like a bunch of maniacs. What happened to Sal is a tragedy, there's no doubt about that, but we're men. We're not animals." He tapped the side of his head. "We need to use our brains as well as our brawn."

"So you want us to do nothing," Randall spat back. "That's typical of you, Huddlestone. You're a man of words, but right now we need action."

"I'm not saying we don't need both," Ignacious said firmly, "but you're all forgetting one big thing that changed round here recently. In fact, it changed just yesterday."

"And what's that?" Randall asked.

"We have a sheriff now," Ignacious pointed out, before turning to look over at Patrick. "Sheriff Cochrane, this seems like something that should be very much in your department. You're our lawman, and that gives you a whole lot of power to decide how we deal with this situation. So, Sheriff, what's it gonna be? Are you gonna lead a group of men out there to get this wolf and any of its brothers and sisters you might find, or do you have another plan in mind?"

Patrick opened his mouth to reply, but in that moment he realized that everyone was watching him, and that they all expected him to come up with the best solution.

"Well, Sheriff?" Randall said, his voice dripping with expectation and enthusiasm. "What's it to be?"

CHAPTER THIRTEEN

Today...

"WELL," AL MAJOR SAID, setting the opened bottle of beer on the counter as everyone in McGinty's fell silent, "there it is. Ladies and gentlemen, the final serving."

As a general hush continued, everyone in the bar stared at the beer. They'd all known that this moment was coming, and Al had been very vocal about the fact that he was fast running out, but now the terrible crisis had arrived. Every single man and woman in the bar wanted that beer, even if it was at room temperature, yet no-one had the temerity to rush forward and grab it; in truth, they all suspected that such an act might well be a crime worthy of an old-fashioned lynching.

"It looks so beautiful," Doug Cooper whispered finally. "Sweet Mary, mother of Jesus, I never truly appreciated a simple bottle of beer until this moment. There's something so utterly spiritual about it. I think I'm having a religious moment."

"It's *just* a bottle of beer," Sindy pointed out.

"So who gets it?" Al asked. "Obviously it's technically mine already, but I think in this deeply important moment we need to think about who deserves it the most. Again, I think I'm pretty high up on that list but -"

Before he could finish, a figure stepped forward and grabbed the bottle, tipping it back and downing the contents in one long swig without giving anyone else a chance to protest. Once he was done, Toby wiped his lips and let out a burp, and then he turned to the others.

"What?" he asked angrily. "Did none of you listen earlier? Have you forgotten everything I've been through over the past couple of days?"

"No-one's forgotten anything," Doug replied.

"You keep telling us often enough," Sindy muttered.

"We're surrounded by wolves," Toby continued, tossing the bottle away, letting it fall onto the floor, "and there's nothing we can do about it. They're biding their time, but their patience is going to wear thin at some point, and then they're going to invade. How do you guys feel about defending yourselves against a full-on wolf attack? What if there are three wolves to every man? They'll rip us to shreds." He pointed toward the bar's front door. "I hope you're not expecting Sheriff Tench to come and save you, because that man is no use at all. He's like a chocolate fireguard."

"So what are you saying, Toby?" Al asked from behind the bar. "Are you saying we're all doomed?"

"I'm saying we need to be cleverer than them," Toby said firmly. "We need to think about what they want, and whether it's in our best interests or not to give it to them."

He paused, and now everyone had fallen silent.

"What if the wolves aren't that crazy?" he continued. "What if they're not evil monsters? What if they can be quite reasonable? What if – and I know this might sound shocking – but what if they actually have a good point?"

"What would that point be?" Murray Andrews asked.

"The wolves want the kid," Toby explained. "As a law enforcement agent, I've been privy to information that the rest of you perhaps didn't receive. But the wolves want Little Miss Dead, or whatever we're calling her now, and I keep wondering to myself... why don't we just hand her over? If she's one of them anyway, or she belongs to them in some way, then why are we risking all our lives just to keep her from them?"

"You want to... turn a little girl over to a bunch of ravenous wolves?" Al asked.

"It's the natural way of things," Toby said, turning to him. "Why should we intervene? A lot of good people have already died to protect that little girl. I watched Sheila die to save her. The same with Megan. The same with a lot of decent people out there in that forest. Zach here can tell you how many good people died facing those wolves, but why did any of it have to happen? Just so we can protect one little girl who doesn't even come from Sobolton? But what if there's an alternative? Here's an idea... if we turned her over to the wolves, they'd leave the rest of us alone."

"It just seems kind of... callous," Sindy suggested. "What if they eat her?"

"Why would they eat her?" he asked. "Now you sound as bad as Tench, tarring those wolves with the same brush like they're a bunch of monsters. If you ask me, they're probably quite civilized. They probably just want the girl back so they can... raise her right. And maybe, just maybe, we've got no good reason to stop them. And let me point out one more thing. Let's say that the wolves *aren't* completely in the right? So what? Why is it our place to try to change that? The Lord can deal with all that stuff. We need to keep our noses out of their business."

He waited, but nobody replied. Looking around at each and every face, he gave them ample chance to argue with him, but each second of silence gave him more confidence and told him that his words had begun to hit home.

"So how about it?" he continued. "Are we gonna cower here, waiting for the wolves to finish us off? Or are we gonna do what's best for us, and what's respectful for the wolf people? Because I know which of those options gets *my* vote."

***

"Marion Bourvoisin keeps asking me to go to her stupid spinning class," Tracy continued, staring into the distance as she sat in the hospital room. "She seems to think that I've got all this spare time at the moment, which is totally the opposite of how my life's going."

She paused, watching the clouds outside.

"People try to be nice," she added, "but they don't have a clue what it's like. They don't realize that I spend every waking hour either doing the school runs or helping with homework or..."

Her voice trailed off again.

"Or coming here to see you," she whispered. "Not that I'm complaining, not for one second. Of course I'm not. It's just that it's all so easy for them when they come to the door. They smile and laugh, and try to cheer me up, and they tell me all about their boring lives as if that's going to distract me from the fact that..."

A shiver ran through her body.

"The fact that our life together has been completely ruined," she said finally. "Because that's the truth, isn't it? Josh has started acting out, I think he blames me for the fact that you're not around at the moment. That's what people don't realize. They always look at the big picture, and they miss all the ways that a life can be destroyed by these tiny little cracks that look small on the surface but go so deep down."

She tilted her head slightly.

"I think -"

"The Walker is on the move," Tommy said suddenly.

Turning, looking at her husband properly for the first time since she'd arrived half an hour earlier, Tracy saw that he was sitting up a little in the bed. Much of his face was still covered in bandages, but now – having remained silent for so long – Tommy's mouth was hanging open.

"What did you say?" she asked.

"The Walker is on the move," he continued. "The Walker is crossing the threshold between worlds. I don't know how, but I... I can just feel it."

"I don't know what you're trying to tell me," she replied, with tears in her eyes. "Tommy, I love you. I've been visiting you as much as I can. Have you even been aware of that?"

"The Walker is leaving Sobolton. Not forever, just to deliver a message. That message will change everything."

"Is that all you've got to say to me?" she asked. "Seriously? Tommy, you're my husband. Can't you talk to me for a moment about normal things?"

"Tell John," he replied, turning to her. "This is important. Tell John that he might already be too late, but tell him... tell him that what he seeks is still here. It might have moved home, but it's still in the town. I don't know how I know these things, but they come to me as clear revelations that burst in my mind. And tell John that soon he'll have to make his choice. Those who are turned can't always switch endlessly between forms. Soon he must decide how to live his life, and his time is already running out."

"I love you," she sobbed. "Tommy, you don't even sound like your real self."

"Tell him that Joe was right," he added. "About everything. Tell him that Joe was right about -"

Suddenly an alarm began to ring out, and Tommy let out a gasp as he fell back against the bed. His body started shaking violently, and Tracy could only watch with a growing sense of horror as two nurses raced into the room and got to work, trying desperately to save him. Voices were shouting and someone was telling her to leave the room, but she felt as if the rest of the world was falling away, leaving her to stare at her dying husband as tears flooded into her eyes and she felt utter sorrow filling the void in her heart.

"He's flat-lining!" a voice yelled somewhere nearby. "Get in here! Hurry!"

CHAPTER FOURTEEN

Sobolton, USA – 1869...

"I WANT EVERY AVAILABLE man ready in ten minutes," Patrick said as he hurried into the office and grabbed one of the rifles. "But we need to be organized. If we're going out there, we have to maintain discipline or we'll get picked off easily enough."

"Hold on just a moment," Ignacious called out breathlessly, as he and Walter finally caught up. "Sheriff Cochrane, are you sure this is the right decision?"

Patrick took a moment to finish preparing the rifle before turning to him.

"This wolf stuff," Ignacious continued, "pops up every now and again, like people can't quite let go of the idea, but you have to understand one thing. Patrick... I mean, Sheriff... I mean... there are no wolves in Sobolton. Or in the area *around* Sobolton."

"Tell that to the dead man."

"I'm not denying that something attacked poor Sal," Ignacious said with a sigh, "but I really don't want to feed this insanity that seems to be gripping the town right now. You're new here, you don't know what it can be like, but there are people in our town who let this fear of wolves whip them up into a frenzy. It's not a good thing."

"Is it true?" Emma McShane asked, rushing into the room and then stopping as soon as she saw Patrick with the rifle. "People are saying there's a wolf, and that a group of men are going to ride out and hunt it down. Is that really happening?"

"Looks that way," Patrick told her. "We've got a convincing report that a wolf was responsible for Sal Weston's death. We can't let that go unchallenged."

"How many men are you taking?" Ignacious asked.

"A dozen ought to do it," Patrick replied.

"A dozen." The older man chewed on that thought for a few seconds. "Seems about reasonable to me. I'm not gonna second guess you, Patrick, because I trust you. That's why I asked you to take on this role in the first place. Just make sure to do this right, because the town can't afford to lose twelve good men."

"Every man who rides out with me today will ride back again," Patrick told him. "You have my word on that."

"Do I get to come?" Walter asked. "Do I get a gun?"

"I need you to stay here and man the fort," Patrick replied. "I know that might be disappointing, Walter, but if I'm out of town you have to stay as my eyes and ears. Do you think you're up to that task?"

"Of course," Walter said, beaming with pride. "Why, I'll be the best eyes and ears you ever had." He turned and hurried out of the room. "People are gonna see that I'm important. I'm finally gonna get the respect I've always deserved."

"What I don't understand," Ignacious muttered, "is why this is all happening *now*. If the wolves have returned – and I'm not saying they have, not yet – but if they have, why have they chosen to come at this particular moment? It just doesn't make any sense."

"Sheriff, might I speak with you alone?" Emma asked. "It's important."

***

"I don't have long," Patrick said as he stepped into a

side-room. "As soon as I've got twelve good men, I need to ride out."

Behind him, Emma gently shut the door. She hesitated, and when she turned to him there was already fear in her eyes.

"I think I know why the wolves might be attacking now," he told her cautiously. "Yesterday I killed those two men in the forest. I brought their heads back but I left their corpses to rot. Now I see that I made a mistake. The wolves probably got a taste for their blood, and then they followed the trail all the way into town." He hesitated for a few seconds. "When you look at it that way," he added, "it's my fault."

"There have *always* been wolves in Sobolton," she told him.

"Ignacious said -"

"I don't care what Ignacious Huddlestone says," she continued, stepping closer to him. "Maybe he's plain wrong, or maybe he's deluding himself. I have no idea. But everyone here knows, if they're honest with themselves, that the wolves never left. There are stories about the old days, stories that a lot of people pretend are just made up, but I truly believe that those stories are true."

"I'm not that interested in stories," he told her. "Stories are for people with too much time on their hands. I'm more interested in what's right in front of me."

"Have you looked at your badge?"

"My -"

Glancing down, Patrick saw the metal badge still fixed to his shirt.

"It's not like other badges," she continued, before slipping a hand into her pocket. She pulled out a simple silver pendant that was hanging from a chain. "This is supposed to be kept in the church," she explained, "but these days nobody cares much about it. It's kept in a drawer. The same people who tell superstitious stories and try to drum up fear... are the same people who leave important relics like this to rot."

"I don't have time to talk about jewelry," Patrick told her. "That's a woman's business."

Fumbling for a moment, Emma finally managed to get the pendant open, revealing the empty space inside.

"This pendant used to contain something very powerful," she explained. "There are different stories about exactly what it was, but some say it was a piece of bone that once belonged to somebody very holy, to someone from the old world. That's the version I like to believe. Nobody knows how it ended up here, but it's said to offer protection to the town. Protection from the wolves."

"Then where is it now?" he asked.

"You're wearing it."

"I'm not sure that I follow."

Stepping over to him, she took a moment to remove the badge from his shirt. Turning it around, she unclipped the back section, allowing her to gently tip a small white chunk of bone into the palm of her hand.

"What exactly am I looking at?" Patrick said cautiously.

"If you believe the stories," she replied in a hushed tone, "it's the piece of bone I just told you about. It might be hundreds and hundreds of years old, and it's extremely powerful. Some people claim that it once was used to save our town from the wolves, when it looked like they might overwhelm us and destroy Sobolton entirely." She held the fragment up so that he could see it more clearly. "I believe that this came from a very holy man. A saint, most likely. And because it's such a holy Christian relic, the wolves can't stand to be around it. Have you noticed something else about your badge?"

"I noticed the slight bulge."

"It's made of silver," she continued. "Somehow this relic, when it was in the silver pendant, became so much more potent against the wolves. A while ago, when people were first talking about finding us a sheriff, my father was charged with making a badge. I knew that the relic was at risk of being lost, but I figured that so long as it remained encased in silver, it can still be powerful.

So I made sure that my father included a place for it in the badge."

She hesitated again, before carefully putting the fragment of bone back into the badge, which in turn she then fixed back onto Patrick's shirt.

"It's of more use like this," she added, "than sitting around in the church. I pray every night that I'm wrong, and that the wolves out there are just ordinary beasts, but I fear that they're far more than that. If they thought our town had been left undefended, they'd come here and slaughter us all, just like they tried in the past. So please, Sheriff Cochrane, take this danger seriously. Better to do that and be wrong, than to laugh it off and... and *then* to be wrong."

"I shall do my duty for this town," he replied, "and let other men decide how much truth there is in these old tales. That sort of thing is really none of my concern, and I don't think I have the right kind of mind to make a pronouncement. But you have my word that I shall deal with any wolves that are out there." Reaching up, he touched the badge. "And the way I see it," he added, "this can only help."

"I hope to see you return soon with good news," she told him.

"Sheriff!" a voice yelled from outside. "We're ready and good to go!"

"I have a job to do," he muttered, looking

into Emma's eyes for a few seconds before stepping past her and heading to the door. As he pulled the door open, he stopped and looked back at her. "Emma McShane, are you married or betrothed?"

"I am not," she replied. "I have had to look after my father for many years."

"I should like to speak to him when I get back," he continued. "With your blessing, I'll ask him his thoughts about maybe... I mean, if you so wish, I need a wife."

"I'm sure he'll agree to that proposition," she said, unable to stifle a faint smile. "I hope so, anyway."

"I'll speak to him upon my return," he said firmly. "For now, Ms. McShane, stay safe and pray for us. I fear we shall need every kind of luck once we get out there and start hunting for wolves."

CHAPTER FIFTEEN

Today...

STANDING ON THE ROOF of a burned-out car, the wolf let out an angry snarl before turning as it caught sight of someone running across the street. The animal hesitated for a fraction of a second before leaping from the car and racing after the woman, quickly biting down hard on the back of her neck and dragging her to the ground.

"Stop!"

Blinking, Doctor Robert Law leaned back in his office chair and tried to put this latest waking nightmare out of his mind. He took a deep breath, trying to calm his racing heart, but he knew that at any moment he might be struck by another of these visions, then another, and that soon he would barely even be able to comprehend the real world behind a veil of ghoulish sights.

Getting to his feet, he leaned on his new cane as he limped around the table. He grabbed a bottle of whiskey from the cabinet, but at the last second he held back as he realized that his hand was shaking. No matter how much he wanted a drink, he figured that he needed to keep a clear head, so after a moment he set the bottle back down and focused instead on trying to keep his hand still. He quickly found that this was much harder than he'd expected.

"Sir?" Cassie said cautiously.

Turning, he saw her standing in the doorway.

"I wouldn't blame you," she continued. "No-one would."

"Can I help you?" he asked, sounding a little more tetchy than he'd intended.

"I tried to find Sheriff Tench, but I'm not quite sure where he is. One of the nurses from the hospital dropped by just now on her way back from work, she thought we should know that Tommy Marshall took a real bad turn. Apparently it's not looking good."

"I was afraid of that," Robert admitted. "That poor bastard's body has been through so much. Even the healthiest heart would struggle."

"She didn't say that he's dead or anything like that," she continued, "just that it's... well, it's not looking so great. I thought you should know."

"Thank you," he murmured, feeling more than ever that he wanted to pour just one glass of whiskey. "I think -"

Before he could finish, they both heard loud voices somewhere in the distance. Turning to look at the window, Robert listened as the voices seemed to come closer, and finally he made his way over and looked out across the parking lot. To his surprise, he saw Toby leading a dozen or more people across the street, heading straight toward the front of the station.

"Damn it," he muttered under his breath. "*Now* what's that fool up to?"

***

"We want the girl!" Toby announced, stopping at the foot of the steps as Robert and Cassie emerged from the station. "We've come to take her."

"What are you talking about?" Robert replied, barely managing to suppress a sense of pure fury. "Toby, you're really surprising me today. Clearly you're even more of an idiot than I realized."

"You can throw insults all you like," Toby continued. "That won't change anything. We're here because we refuse to see our town get dragged down just because of one girl. We don't have anything against Elsie or Elisa or whatever her name is, but we all recognize that things have gotten worse and worse since she was pulled out of the ice. Now we've got no power, no way of contacting the outside world, no running water or sanitation -"

"No beer," Doug added.

"And we're just sitting around waiting for wolves to come and rip us to pieces," Toby added. "We're decent people, we're not cruel or mean, but enough's enough. We're going to take that little girl and hand her over peacefully to the wolves, and then in return they'll leave us alone."

"Are you serious?" Robert snarled. "What the hell has happened to all of you? Is this really all it takes to turn you into a gang of barbarians?"

"Again with the insults," Toby replied. "You can't engage on the actual topic, Doctor Law, so you sling rude comments. Frankly, I'd have hoped that a doctor might be above such things."

"Can the manufactured outrage," Robert said darkly, before looking at other people in the crowd. "Doug Cooper, I never thought I'd see you joining a baying mob. Or you, Jerome Mackenzie. And you, Miriam, what the hell are you doing with these people? Some of you show up to church every Sunday, claiming to be good people, and now suddenly you want to literally throw an innocent little girl to a pack of wolves?"

"Who says she's innocent?" a voice called

out from the crowd.

"Exactly," Toby continued. "Doctor Law, I'm sure you're very good at your job, cutting people up and suchlike, but this is a matter of principle and I'm not sure that's really your area of expertise."

"Oh, you're not, huh?" Robert said, raising both eyebrows. "Well, that's awfully brave of you to say, Toby. You really seem to be in the mood for sharing your opinions today, no matter how moronic they might be."

"I'm not joining you in the gutter, Doctor Law," Toby replied. "I'd like to think that we're all above that sort of thing. We're here for the girl, and we're not going to leave without her, so you might as well hand her over."

Before he could reply, Robert spotted John on the other side of the street, approaching with Lisa and Eloise in tow.

"You want to take Eloise and give her to the wolves?" Robert called out loudly, causing John and the others to immediately stop in their tracks. "Well, we're not going to let you do that. There's no way I'm just going to bring Eloise out of this station and give her to you, and I sure hope you're not planning on storming in here to try to take her."

He saw John leading Lisa and Eloise away, and he felt a flicker of relief that at least he'd managed to warn them before they'd been seen by anyone in the crowd. Sometimes, just sometimes, plans actually worked.

"Don't make us do this the hard way," Toby said firmly. "We're patient, Doctor Law, but nobody's patience lasts forever. We'll give you a little time to think things through, and to hopefully come to the right conclusion, but eventually we're going to have to force the issue. We don't want violence or confrontation. We don't even want to stoop to name-calling. We're simply concerned citizens who have a right to express their thoughts on this process, and we all agree that we can't keep going on like this. Something has to give. Little Miss Dead has to go back to her own people in the forest. We have no right to keep her from them."

"He's right!" a voice yelled from the back of the crowd.

A murmur of agreement spread through the group.

"Well, you're not getting her," Robert announced. "We're going to lock the doors to the station, and I'd like to remind you that anyone who attempts to break into the place will face serious criminal charges." Turning, he headed back to the door. "Come on, Cassie," he added, "we -"

Suddenly something hit his shoulder with a thud. Shocked, he turned just as a small rock tumbled down onto the ground.

"Who threw that?" he shouted.

"I didn't see," Toby replied with a grin, "but

I certainly don't condone violence. You have to understand, though, that we're just the common men and women of Sobolton and we're angry that our voices aren't being heard. You and Sheriff Tench have had ample time to deal with this situation, and you've only made it worse and worse. The sun's gonna set in a few hours, and none of us can handle another night of darkness and fear. I guess that counts as a kind of deadline, Doctor Law. Turn the girl over to us by the time the shadows start getting too long, or one way or the other we're coming in there to get her. You don't think you can stop us, do you?"

"Get inside," Robert said, opening the door and stepping back into the station.

He waited until Cassie had joined him, and then he shut the door and made sure to lock it properly. Having only recently been repaired, however, the door was already far from sturdy.

"Secure every other door and window as best you can," he said through gritted teeth as he looked at the crowd waiting outside.

"Of course," Cassie replied nervously, "but... Sir, Eloise isn't here, so why don't you just tell them that?"

"Because at least right now we've got their attention focused in the wrong location," he explained, keeping his eyes fixed on Toby. "They're not going to storm the station, not really. They're a bunch of cowards. All we have to do is keep them yelling at us, so that John and Lisa have time out there to come up with a better plan."

CHAPTER SIXTEEN

Sobolton, USA – 1869...

"ARE WE SURE WE'RE heading in the right direction?" Randall asked, as Patrick led the posse away from Sobolton and out through a section of the forest that ran close to the lake. "How do we know the wolves are round here?"

"We don't," Patrick admitted, "but I've got a hunch that this is connected to what happened yesterday."

He was already watching the ground ahead closely, hoping that he would manage to find the right spot again.

"I shouldn't have left those two corpses out here," he continued. "My worry is that by doing that, I might have caused the wolves to come closer.

If they were attracted by the scent, they might have become emboldened."

"So you're saying this is all your fault?" Randall replied.

Patrick turned to him.

"Just a little joke there, Sheriff," Randall continued with a big, broad grin. "I wasn't meaning to needle you or anything like that."

Ignoring him entirely, Patrick focused his attention on the path ahead. For the next few minutes the men rode mostly in silence, before finally Patrick stopped as he spotted what remained of a man's pelvis and legs.

"Hold up!" he called out, before dismounting and taking a closer look.

"Is that one of them?" Andy Munroe called out. "Is that one of those bandits you killed?"

"It is," Patrick replied, using his foot to turn the pelvis over, quickly seeing that some of the clothing had been torn away. The flesh was ripped and in places almost shredded, and sure enough he saw various dismembered organs spread out across the ground nearby. "They weren't like this when I left them, though," he added, stepping over the pelvis and inspecting a bloodied liver that had been left on the rocks. "If the wolves had been starving, even just hungry, they'd have consumed every part of these men," he continued. "Instead they pulled them apart, like they were playing with them."

Spotting another set of similarly destroyed remains nearby, he realized that his worst fears had now been confirmed. The two corpses had evidently attracted the wolves' attention and, in turn, probably had a lot to do with Sal Weston and Paul May running into one of the creatures when they'd ventured out of the forest. Looking around, Patrick saw no sign of any wolves now, yet deep down he felt sure that they had to be nearby. At the same time, given the curve of the lake, he supposed that they must have come from further along the shoreline, and already he was trying to figure out exactly where their natural territory might be located. He figured that there had to be a wolf heartland somewhere.

"This doesn't feel right," Andy said after a moment. "I feel like we're somewhere we shouldn't be."

The others turned to him.

"Don't you feel it too?" he continued. "Man, I'm feeling almost itchy here. It's like my body's reacting to something in the air."

"Calm yourself down," Paul May murmured. "The last thing we need right now is to have some damn fool panicking."

"I'm not panicking!" Andy hissed. "I'm reacting to something that's totally obvious. I don't get how the rest of you can't sense it!"

"I think I know what you mean," Patrick

told him. "I was out here yesterday, and already something seems to have changed." He looked around again, trying to work out exactly what he was sensing, but the forest appeared fairly safe and he worried that he might be imagining things. "We're going to keep going for another hour, and see how things look," he continued. "Any man who wants to turn back is more than welcome to do so, with no recriminations. But I want to get a better idea of what we might be facing."

He turned to look back at the others.

"Who's with me?"

***

Around one hour later, with only Andy Munroe having taken up the offer to turn around, Patrick and the rest of the men reached a clearing in the forest that led all the way down to the lake's shore. Stopping once more, Patrick looked around but still saw nothing that indicated wolf activity.

"Well?" Billy Chambers called out from the rear of the posse. "Now what?"

"We haven't seen so much as a pile of wolf shit," Randall Pierce pointed out. "I think we're going in completely the wrong direction."

"Wait," Patrick replied, climbing down from Blackspot and stepping over to something he'd spotted on the ground. Picking it up, he found that he was holding a human arm bone that had been almost entirely stripped of flesh. "This can't be too old," he continued, turning around and showing it to the others. "I think one of the wolves carried it all this way after picking those bandits apart."

"Why would it do that?"

"I don't know," Patrick replied, looking ahead again, only to quickly spot another piece of bone. Making his way over, he picked up a chunk that turned out to be from a man's sternum, and already he could see more fragments not too far away. "Looks like they dropped quite a lot when they came this way. It's almost as if -"

Before he could finish, a wolf's howl rang out, filling the air.

Every member of the posse drew their guns, as Patrick looked around and tried to work out exactly where the howl had come from. Silence had already returned, but now any last lingering suspicion about the wolves – or lack thereof – had faded and he knew for certain what they were all facing.

"What do we think, gentlemen?" Randall asked, and now his voice was positively dripping with sarcasm. "Was that a wolf, or could it maybe have been an itty bitty squirrel?"

Patrick turned to him, ready to tell him to shut up, but in that moment another wolf howled. This time the sound was much closer, seemingly coming from back the way the men had just come.

"Was that behind us?" Billy asked fearfully. "Are they behind us now?"

"If they've circled round us," Randall said, watching the trees carefully, "that seems awful smart for a bunch of dumb critters."

"These bones," Patrick said cautiously, "are arranged almost in a line. It's almost as if someone placed them here very deliberately in an attempt to draw us in this direction so that -"

Stopping suddenly, he looked around again. He and the other men were standing in a natural dip, with the forest rising up high on three sides and the lake cutting them off to the south. From his time in the army, he was familiar with attempts to gain a strategic advantage, and already his mind was racing as he began to realize that he'd allowed them all to be lured into a perfect ambush situation. Watching the trees, he waited for any hint of movement, and sure enough after just a few seconds his worst fears were realized.

A lone wolf was slinking between two of the trees, apparently unworried about being spotted.

Turning to look the other way, Patrick saw another wolf in a different part of the forest.

"There!" Randall yelled, aiming in yet another direction and firing twice, hitting a distant tree and sending two wolves scurrying away.

"That's four so far," Patrick whispered, still

trying desperately to get a good read of the situation. A moment later he spotted two more wolves, then another. "Seven."

"We've got 'em outnumbered, though, right?" Billy said cautiously. "Sheriff, isn't that right? There are still more of us than there are them."

"Eight," Patrick continued, counting under his breath as he saw more and more wolves beyond the treeline. "Ten. Fourteen. Eighteen."

"I'm not liking this," Randall said, turning to look in every direction but seeing wolves everywhere, as if the creatures were starting to slowly bleed out of the forest. "They don't seem very scared. How many of them are there?"

"A lot," Patrick muttered. "Hold your fire for a moment."

"Are you insane?" Randall shouted.

"I said, hold your fire!" Patrick continued. "They're doing this for a reason. They're showing themselves because they *want* us to waste our bullets on hopeless shots. They want us emptying our guns while they're still far away, and then they can move in for the kill."

"They're wolves!" Randall snapped. "They're just dumb animals! They're not capable of coming up with plans like that!"

"Unless you believe some of the other stories about them," Joseph Ward said. "Come on, we've all heard the tales. Some people reckon these wolves aren't *just* wolves, that they're as smart as people. Some even claim that they can change and look like us. What if that's what these things are? What if they're wolves with the smarts of men?"

"Don't talk rubbish!" Randall replied.

"How many are there?" Billy whimpered, clearly close to tears now as he looked all around. "Sheriff, how many wolves are there?"

"Too many," Patrick said, watching as more and more wolves emerged from the forest in every direction. Already, he could tell that the creatures were in no way fearful, and that he and the rest of the posse were hopelessly outnumbered. "A hundred. More, even. There are hundreds and hundreds of the damn things."

CHAPTER SEVENTEEN

Today...

"ARE THOSE PEOPLE INSANE?" Lisa asked, keeping hold of Eloise's hand as she followed John along another street. "What did Bob mean about them taking Eloise?"

"It's Toby again," John muttered, still struggling to come up with a decent plan. "He has a particular talent when it comes to riling people up, and evidently he's up to his usual tricks again. I swear, when this mess is over, if we get out of it alive... I'm going to make sure he rots away in a jail cell."

"Why are people mad at me?" Eloise asked.

"Honey, they're not mad at you," Lisa explained. "You haven't done anything wrong, okay? It's just that there are some very bad people around, and some of them have... strange ideas. Ideas that we really don't need to listen to."

"We need to find somewhere to hide out for a few hours," John said, stopping at the next corner and looking all around. "My place is too obvious, and so's yours. We can't go to Bob, but there has to be someone we can turn to."

"We need to get back to Rachel's place."

"That might be too far," he said, turning to her. "Toby's going to have people watching the streets. Even if he's convinced that Eloise is at the station, he's going to be putting feelers out just in case. We need somewhere nearby, somewhere nobody's going to think of and somewhere we can reach without drawing attention to ourselves."

"I have an idea," Lisa told him. "It's close to the station, but there's a way around the back so we should be able to get in without any trouble." She paused for a moment. "It's not the least obvious place in the world, but it's been empty for a long time so... I think it might just work."

***

"I can't believe this place has just been left to rot," Lisa said once she'd climbed through the window, entering a corridor at the rear of her old veterinary surgery. "I know there were probably complications thanks to my disappearance, but still..."

Stopping for a moment, she listened for any hint of movement, but she was already fairly certain that the place was empty. This particular corridor ran between the examinations rooms and the front office, and she couldn't help but think back not only to her own time in charge but also to the days when her father had worked in the building. Most of her life had been closely linked to the surgery, to the extent that now she felt almost as if she was finally home.

Behind her, John and Eloise had finally managed to make their way inside too.

"Are you sure this isn't too obvious?" he asked, keeping his voice low. "This place literally has your family's name out the front."

"You mean that faded old sign? I really don't think that anyone's going to look in here. Plus, if they do, we'll see them coming across the parking lot and we can easily get out the back. All things considered, I'd rather be in here than still wandering around outside." She took Eloise's hand again and led her along the corridor. "I'm pretty sure that Bob tricked the crowd. It'll be a while before they even think to come looking somewhere like this."

"By the time that happens," John replied as he followed her, "we need to be gone. This is only a temporary pit stop while we come up with a way to deal with this mess."

"Rachel said the equipment was sold off to cover a few debts," she said, glancing into empty rooms as she made her way past. "It's so strange to see the place like this. While I was in the cabin, I longed to get back eventually, but now that I'm here..."

Reaching the door that led into the reception area, she felt a whole fresh pang of sadness. She spotted some old papers that had been left on the counter, so she wandered over and took a look.

"Huh," she said as soon as she recognized the details on the top page. "Bruce the guinea pig. Norman's little guy. I'm sure Bruce is long gone by now, but I guess he might have some descendants kicking around. I wonder if anyone ever worked out what was causing his little ear to get infected so often."

Heading to the window, John peered through a gap in the blinds and saw the crowd outside the station. He couldn't be sure, but he felt fairly sure that the crowd had already grown a little, and he saw more people watching from the other side of the street. For now, Toby's rebellion was limited to a couple of dozen malcontents, but John knew full well that the situation could rapidly get much worse. Night would start to fall soon, and the accompanying darkness was likely to make everything far more feverish. He understood why people might turn violent as the food began to run out, and as associated problems – lack of power, lack of sanitation, lack of water – became more extreme.

A moment later, a figure near the back of the crowd turned and looked directly toward the surgery. Pulling back slightly, John worried that he might have been spotted, even if he felt sure that he was too far away. The figure watched for a few more seconds, before finally turning to look back at the others. For now, at least, Lisa's theory seemed to be holding true.

"We need to fix this before it gets dark out there," he said, turning to her.

"Eloise," Lisa replied, turning to her daughter, "can you go through into that back room there, just for a minute or two? I need to speak to John and I'm sure you'd find it all very boring. There are some books through there that we used to keep for kids in the waiting room. Looks like they're still there, so why don't you take a look through them and see if anything catches your fancy?"

"Okay," Eloise said, clearly not too convinced as she headed through the doorway behind the counter.

"What we're doing now isn't working," Lisa continued, making her way over to John, keeping her voice down so that her daughter wouldn't be able to hear. "Obviously we're not handing her over to Saint Thomas and the wolves, and it's not like they're going to back down, so there's only one solution."

"We *have* to get you guys out of here," he admitted.

"For now, the wolves are managing to keep us cut off from the rest of the world. That's clever of them, but there comes a point when someone *has* to notice that an entire town is basically missing. I don't know how long it's going to take, but sooner or later people will come knocking hard on Sobolton's door, and the wolves know that too. There's no way they'll let us get through another night like this."

"Agreed."

"Do you know about the bunkers?"

"What bunkers?"

"I wish I'd paid more attention at the time," she continued, "but when I was growing up, everyone at school used to talk about these bunkers in the forest. I don't know how you get into them, but the story goes that they were built during the Cold War as a possible place for people to hide away. That means they're deep underground and they're protected."

"How does that help us?"

"If we can get Eloise down into one of them, there's a chance that the wolves can be tricked into believing that she's gone. If she's that far underground, in a bunker that's designed to protect people from nuclear fallout, doesn't it stand to reason that it might shield her scent from the wolves as well? If they genuinely think that she's gone, if we can hide the scent leading out there, why would they bother continuing with their attack on the town?"

"Revenge?"

"Not worth it for them," she replied quickly. "At least, not based on everything Michael ever told me. The wolves don't actually want all-out war, not if they can help it. They know that if they draw too much attention to themselves, outside forces like the U.S. government might start to ask questions. They want to stay under the radar, so we just need to give them an off-ramp from what they're doing at the moment."

"How can we get to these bunkers?" he asked. "How do we even know where they are? I don't know about you, but I don't much like the idea of wandering aimlessly round the forest in the hope that we find one. I've been out there a fair amount and I've never spotted hatches or anything like that."

"There'll be records," she told him. "I don't even think that they're *that* secret, although I imagine that the wolves don't know about them."

"I'm guessing these records are unlikely to be found in an abandoned veterinary facility."

"Sure, but they'll be in some combination of your station and the town hall."

"Which are both right in the firing line of that angry mob," he pointed out. "Even if what you're saying is true, there's no way for us to get to them. The moment we go out there and head anywhere near either of those locations, we'll be spotted instantly."

"There might be a way," she told him, before hesitating for a few more seconds. "But... you're really not going to like it."

CHAPTER EIGHTEEN

Sobolton, USA – 1869...

"DID YOU HEAR THAT?" Sarah Higgins asked, looking up from the tin bath she was using to wash some clothes. "I heard another one!"

"Don't let them get to you," Emma replied as she hung another shirt from the line. "Sheriff Cochrane and the others are out there now, and they'll deal with the problem."

"How can you be so sure?" Sarah asked. "The man arrived yesterday! We have no idea whether or not he's up to the task!"

"I have faith in him," Emma said firmly. "I can't explain it, but I can tell that he's a good man, and that he'll make the right move at the right time."

"He doesn't know what he's up against,"

Sarah continued. "You know the old tales as well as I do, Emma. You know that those wolves aren't *just* wolves."

"Of course I do," she replied, "but panicking won't help anyone."

"You also know that there are likely to be far more of them out there," Sarah pointed out. "A dozen men, no matter how strong and brave, will be no match if they're hopelessly outnumbered. What if we've simply sent our best men to get slaughtered? That would leave us completely undefended, and then those *things* could come and pick us off whenever they're ready."

"Sobolton's a decent-sized town," Emma pointed out, drying her hands. "Maybe there was a time, back in the day, when we'd be vulnerable to something like that, but now we're much stronger. We've still got plenty of good, strong men around who know how to put up a fight." She stepped around the tin bath and began to head to the front of the house. "Sheriff Cochrane and the others will be back soon, have no doubt about that. And they'll be bringing good news."

As if to immediately undermine that point, another howl rang out in the distance, far beyond the edge of town.

"I hope she's right," a voice said, and Sarah turned to see Octavia Willoughby leaning on a nearby fence, having evidently listened to the whole conversation, "but I can't help thinking about something my grandfather used to tell me. His grandfather, or maybe great-grandfather, was one of the early settlers here, and he passed down a story about something known as a Walker."

"Everyone knows that story," Sarah replied.

"Yes, but they don't all take it seriously," Octavia continued. "Not as seriously as it *should* be taken, at least. I don't hear many people talking about it these days, but how do we know that those wolves don't still have one of their own living here in the town? How do we know that there isn't a wolf in a man's form?" She paused for a few seconds. "Or a woman's form..."

"What are you driving at?" Sarah asked with a sigh.

"I'm driving at the idea that the wolves have got their spy in our midst, and it's probably someone we'd never think to suspect. Someone who looks the exact opposite to a wolf."

"I don't know who you could possibly mean," Sarah insisted.

"I'm not pointing a finger at you, Sarah," Octavia replied. "I'm just thinking that young Emma there seemed mighty unconcerned about those howls we're all hearing. If you ask me, she spends too much time poking her nose into everyone else's business, like she has this need to find out what's going on all the time. Almost like she's gathering information so she can relay it to others."

"You can't be serious," Sarah said. "That girl is good and pious."

"She *acts* good and pious," Octavia added, "but it's not just me thinking it. A lot of people have begun to wonder, although so far they only whisper. But Emma goes off by herself sometimes, out into the forest. She says she's going out collecting mushrooms, but she'd sure have the time and opportunity to meet up with someone out there." A faint smile reached her lips. "I was born in Sobolton and, God willing, I'll die here too. I've never even left the town boundary. And I sure hate the idea that we might be sitting around, twiddling our thumbs while a bunch of wolves plan their big attack. If you ask me, we need to get ahead of this fast."

She leaned a little further over the fence, and now she could see the fear and doubt in Sarah's eyes.

"If there's another Walker in this town," she continued, "we need to flush that beast out. And fast!"

***

"An unclean beast walking among us?" Father Vacelli said, standing in the church and staring at the altar for a moment, before slowly turning to the handful of concerned townsfolk who'd arrived to speak with him. "Walking on its hind legs and speaking with a man's tongue?"

"Or a woman," Octavia said firmly. "Don't forget that. It could be a woman."

"I find it hard to credit such an idea," the priest continued. "How would this deception be perpetrated for any length of time?"

"I think," Sarah said cautiously, "the idea is that they're quite intelligent. That they can disguise their sinfulness and pretend to be good."

"One must always be aware of such dangers," Vacelli replied, "but in this case I fail to see any evidence."

"It's Emma McShane," Octavia said firmly.

"I beg your pardon?"

"Everyone knows it," Octavia continued, warming to her theme now. "She has the motive and the opportunity. She's the Walker and she's feeding information back to her fellow wolves. She goes out into the forest, pretending to be picking mushrooms, but she never returns with more than a handful. I've seen how plentifully those mushrooms grow even at the very edge of the forest, so why does she never return with a fully laden basket? I'll tell you why! It's because she's spending all her time conversing with her brethren!"

"Are we sure that we're not getting carried away?" Vacelli asked.

"It's true about the basket," Mary Strine said nervously. "I've seen it myself. I always wondered why she was so unlucky, but... I didn't realize the explanation until now."

"If she's innocent," Octavia added, "she oughta be able to prove it. You're a priest, Father Vacelli. You must know how to draw the evil out of her."

"There are ways," he admitted cautiously, "but -"

"The Lord would want us to move fast," Octavia continued. "I never told anyone this before, I didn't want to cause fear, but lately I've been having the most terrifying visions of what might happen to us if we let the wolves overrun us. And the worst part is that sometimes in these visions, I see Emma McShane in the heart of all the chaos and... she's laughing!"

"I find that difficult to imagine," Vacelli said calmly.

"You won't *have* to imagine it if she gets her way," Octavia explained. "Haven't you noticed the way she is when she talks to the rest of us? She's so eager to please, so keen to seem like a nice person. She's acting the role of a decent citizen, but that's all it is. An act. I sensed something wrong with her from the moment I first set eyes on her, although I confess that it took me some time to suspect the truth. I can only hope that the Lord forgives me for this lackadaisical failure."

"Well," Vacelli replied, trying to pick his words with care, "that is certainly one view on the matter but -"

"It's the only view!" Octavia snapped, momentarily showing her anger before quickly taking a moment to restrain herself. "I'm sorry to raise my voice around you, Father. It was not my intention to show any disrespect, but I believe so strongly in the Lord's work and I quiver at the thought of this impostor causing us so much trouble."

"I would remind you," he said cautiously, "that these accusations might well be without merit. I myself have seen nothing to suggest that Emma means any of us harm."

"Then you must devise a test for her," Octavia continued, as if she had already thought ahead to this argument and was determined to head it off. "I have already come up with one, if it would please you to listen. I remember the old stories about the Walker, and it was said that the beast's skin was particularly sensitive. Since it was not in its natural shape, the Walker would cry out in pain if its skin was in any way disturbed. I believe we can use this fact to our advantage. If you are amenable, I shall set up a fair and true test that will settle the matter once and for all."

"I am really not sure about this," the priest

told her.

"Emma shall have a chance to prove her innocence," Octavia explained, "and I shall have an equal chance to prove her guilt. And nobody shall be able to complain about the result. But let me say this, Father. If she proves to be what I think she is... we must act fast!"

CHAPTER NINETEEN

Today...

AFTER TAKING A MOMENT – a moment too long, perhaps – to carefully fold his shirt, John set it down on the chair in the corner of the old reception room.

"Are you ready?" Lisa asked from the doorway.

"I don't know," he replied, shocked by the fear in his own voice. Turning, he saw that she was half in the room and half out, and that she was half watching him and half trying to avert her gaze. He didn't blame her for that at all.

"Eloise is in one of the other rooms," she continued. "I don't want her to see this."

He nodded.

"She says you'll be able to feel the moment when you let go," she added. "She says it shouldn't be that difficult for you to sense it. To be honest, I was shocked when she said all of that. I had no idea that she was also struggling to... contain herself."

"I don't even know that this will work," John told her. "There might be a better plan if we just -"

"We don't have time for anything else," she insisted, interrupting him. "You've already told me about your doubts, and I understand them, but time's running out. Please, John, I'm begging you to help. I know Eloise is nothing to you, she's not your blood, but you can't possibly want that baying mob to get their hands on her."

"If there's one thing I hate," he replied, "it's a mob."

"Eloise says you'll have the clarity you need," she continued. "It's such a crazy idea, but the plan will work if we just stick to it. We'll meet you at the arranged point, and so long as you have the information we need about those bunkers..."

Her voice trailed off.

"Or is it a total disaster?" she added. "It's so convoluted, it could go wrong at any moment and -"

"It won't go wrong," he replied. "I *can* feel how to do it. I've been holding it back for a while now, and Eloise is right... I know how to stop pushing against it. I don't know how long it'll take to work, and I apologize in advance if I do or say anything shocking." He took a deep breath. "I think it's already starting. Would you mind... not watching? I want to have a little privacy and dignity. I get the feeling that this is going to be a wild ride."

"Good luck," she told him, with tears in her eyes.

She hesitated, before starting to shut the door.

"Oh, and Lisa?" he continued. "Please don't forget my clothes. I really don't want to be sneaking through town naked again."

She nodded, and then she shut the door just as he turned away and began to pull down his underwear. Once she was alone in the corridor, she leaned back against the wall and waited. Her heart was racing and she felt that the entire plan was an impossible mess that hinged on one too many improbable turns, yet she also knew that there was no alternative. She knew that John was making a huge sacrifice for her – and for Eloise – and she could only hope that this sacrifice would not be in vain.

A moment later, hearing a cracking sound coming from the reception area, she let out a gasp. On the other side of the door, John let out a low, pained grunt – as if he was in desperate agony. Clenching her teeth, Lisa resisted the urge to rush back into the room, but finally she got down onto her knees and tried to peer through the keyhole. At first she could see nothing, but after altering her angle a little she finally spotted something moving in the room. And as she heard a sickening splitting sound accompanied by a groan of pain, she realized that the transformation had begun.

Although she couldn't quite make out the shape she was seeing through the keyhole, she could already tell that it was no longer human.

***

"Goddamn pompous asshole," Toby muttered darkly, watching the silhouette of Doctor Robert Law in the station's window. "When I get my hands on that prick, I'm gonna teach him a lesson he'll never forget."

"Toby?"

Startled, he turned to see that Zach had made his way over.

"People are starting to ask how much longer we're gonna wait," Zach continued. "It's getting late and everyone's hungry and -"

"Hungry?" Toby spat back at him. "We're trying to save our town, and people are moaning and bitching about being hungry? Are you serious?"

"I'm just reporting what the others are telling me," Zach replied, holding both his hands up. "We've been here for a couple of hours now and... well, nothing much seems to be happening. And it'll be getting dark in another hour or so, so people are wondering if we're going to let this drag on into the night. Also, nobody thought to bring flashlights, and even if they did, people are running low on batteries and -"

"Don't talk to me about batteries!" Toby snapped angrily, before stepping past him and seeing that the small crowd was already starting to dissipate. "Am I surrounded by utter buffoons?"

"It's late," Doug said, turning to follow a few others who'd already begun to walk off. "I'm going to McGinty's. At least the place still *smells* of beer and -"

Suddenly a cry rang out, followed by a scream, and the crowd began to move back en masse to the steps at the front of the sheriff's station. Toby watched them, for a moment not understanding what was making them panic, but after a few seconds he realized that they were all looking at a spot behind him. Even Zach was backing away now, and when he turned to look Toby saw to his horror that a large grayish wolf was slowly padding across the edge of the parking lot, steadily making its way closer.

"It's one of them!" Zach shouted. "Are there more? Are they attacking?"

Looking all around, Toby expected to see

more wolves, but so far there seemed to be only the one lone specimen.

"What do we do?" a man in the crowd asked.

Filled with a sense of panic, Toby felt frozen to the spot for a few seconds, until the wolf edged closer and began to let out a rumbling snarl. Convinced that this snarl was personal, and that the wolf somehow hated him in particular, Toby turned and hurried over to the group, slipping past them before stopping to take refuge behind a group of women.

"Keep it away from me!" he hissed. "It's coming for me! Did you see the way it looked at me? It knows I'm the leader and it wants to take me out!"

Nobody dared to speak as the wolf made its way past. The animal was clearly trying to keep as far back as possible, while watching the group and occasionally baring its fangs as if to offer a warning. Making its way slowly across the parking lot, the wolf walked with an unusual stiffness that seemed to hint that it was constantly poised to leap into action, and the people at the front of the gathering began to step back in an attempt to maintain as much distance as possible.

And then, with no warning, the wolf turned and bolted, racing away across the other end of the parking lot and quickly disappearing behind the town hall.

"What's it doing?" Sindy asked. "Where's it going?"

"I think it's by itself," Lou Simmons added. "Is it... checking us out? Do you think it's some kind of scout that was sent ahead to see what we're doing?"

"That thing had murder in its eyes," Toby sneered as he finally realized that the immediate danger had passed. Stepping out from behind the women, he took a moment to adjust the collar of his shirt, which was starting to feel far too tight. "You all saw the way it looked at me! It came to kill me, and it's a miracle I survived!"

The others turned to him.

"That's a sign that we're doing the right thing," he continued. "You all see that, right? The wolf came to try to scare us off, because it knows that we're starting to organize properly."

"Why would it want to scare us off?" Doug asked, having abandoned his plan to return to McGinty's. "Doesn't it want us to get the little girl and hand her over?"

"I can't explain every little bit of its intentions," Toby replied. "I'm not a mind reader, especially when it comes to wolves. But our plan still stands, and it's obvious that we need to get a move on!"

"But -"

"No more arguments!" he snapped angrily, turning and looking at the front door of the station. "We've let that asshole doctor hold us back for long enough! The time has come for us to force the issue. That little girl is in this building, and we're going to take her. And if Law and his buddies won't hand her over willingly, that leaves us with only one other option!"

CHAPTER TWENTY

Sobolton, USA – 1869...

"WE'RE SURROUNDED BY HUNDREDS and hundreds of wolves and you *don't* want us to start shooting?" Randall asked, struggling to hold back his fear. "Sheriff, with all due respect... have you completely lost your mind?"

"How many shots have we got left combined?" Patrick asked, keeping his eyes fixed on the wolves that even now were still slowly emerging from the forest. "And how many wolves are there?"

"There must be two hundred by now," Billy said, barely able to speak at all as his teeth chattered with fear. "And more every second."

"Exactly," Patrick continued. "We don't

have enough ammunition to take them all down, even if a single shot would do for each of them and even if we don't miss at all. So if we shoot all over the place, at best we'll take down only a few of them, and whatever's left'll be all riled up and thirsty for revenge."

"So what's the plan?" Randall replied. "Do you want us to just sit here and wait to die?"

Patrick opened his mouth to reply, but for a few seconds he genuinely wasn't sure what to say. He'd been in a few difficult spots before, back when he'd been fighting in the war, and from experience he believed that there was always a way to find victory; at the same time, he worried that he was biased due to the fact that he'd always managed to survive, and he figured that for some men there came a time when they couldn't do a damn thing to save their own lives.

A moment later, feeling a tugging sensation on the front of his shirt, he looked down and saw that his badge was trembling slightly.

"What the..."

"I'm out of here!" Billy yelled suddenly, pulling on his horse's reins, turning the animal around and starting to gallop away. "I'm too young to die out here!"

"Wait!" Patrick shouted angrily. "Don't be a fool!"

Ignoring him, Billy rode toward the treeline,

clearly attempting to follow the trail back to town. Before he could get anywhere near the trees, however, three wolves lunged at his horse, biting the animal's legs and bringing cries of pain from its mouth as it stumbled and fell.

"He's down!" Randall snarled, and now he too turned his horse around. "We've got a man down!"

"Don't break formation!" Patrick told him, but already a couple of other men were also riding to Billy's aid. "Listen to me! It won't work!"

In that moment Billy let out a scream, and Patrick realized that he had no choice but to follow the others. Riding Blackspot back across the open space, he saw to his horror that several wolves had now rushed to Billy and were tearing at him, pulling on his limbs as if they intended to rip him to pieces.

A shot rang out, then another, as Randall and a couple of men fired at the beasts. Patrick saw at least a couple of the bullets hitting the wolves' flanks, but – as he'd suspected – the animals showed no sign that they were even being slowed down.

"Stop wasting your ammunition!" Patrick shouted, but already some of the other men were firing too. To his horror, he saw that a number of the shots had hit Billy. "You're missing! Can't you see it with your own eyes? You're killing him!"

He drew his own gun, but he knew he had to try to stay calm. As the other men cried out to one another and continued firing, Patrick finally climbed down from his horse and began to make his way over. He still wasn't quite sure what he was going to do, but a moment later he saw that he was already too late. The wolves had begun to tear Billy apart, ripping his legs away and letting blood gush out onto the rocky ground.

With his chest already riddled with bullet wounds, Billy was still just about alive, screaming in agony as the wolves continued their attack. After a few seconds, Patrick raised his gun and took a moment to aim, and then he fired; the shot hit Billy in the forehead, blowing one side of his head clean away but at least ending his pain.

"What did you do that for?" Randall shouted, turning to Patrick and raising his gun. "You killed him!"

"He was dead already," Patrick snarled. "He was dead the moment he turned and tried to get away, and if we're not very careful we'll all end up the same."

Randall hesitated, as if he was genuinely considering pulling the trigger, but finally he lowered the gun. He turned, and the men all watched for a few seconds as the wolves continued to ferociously rip the dead man's body apart, spilling his stomach and liver across the stones but making no obvious attempt to actually eat any of the bloodied pieces.

"It's like I said," Patrick continued as he looked around and saw more and more wolves circling their position. "They're not doing this to feed. They're doing this to send us a message, or even just because they enjoy it. Probably a little of both."

"Then how do we stop them?" Randall snapped.

Feeling the same tugging sensation on his shirt as before, Patrick looked down to see that his badge was shaking harder, and this time he was just about able to make out a faint rattling sound coming from inside. He thought back to the small piece of bone, and to everything Emma had told him, and finally he began to unpin the badge.

"What are you doing?" Randall asked. "Are you surrendering? Are you abandoning us?"

"Get out of my way," Patrick replied, shoving him aside as he hurried toward the wolves that even now were still dismembering what remained of Billy's corpse.

"He's a coward!" Randall shouted to the others. "Are you watching this? He's a coward and he's gonna run away!"

"The only ones who are gonna run are these wolves," Patrick sneered, reaching the spot where Billy had fallen and holding the badge out. "This had better work!"

A fraction of a second later one of the

wolves turned and snarled at him, but the creature then pulled back; still snarling, the beast seemed terrified of Patrick's approach. Sure enough, as he turned and held the badge out toward the rest of the wolves, they too began to back away. Despite continued growls, the creatures were clearly terrified, and Patrick found that he was able to easily force them away until eventually they all turned and ran back to join the rest of the pack.

"Do you see this?" Patrick shouted, still holding the badge up as he turned to look at the hundreds of wolves now encircling the posse. "You know what it is, don't you? And you know what it can do to you!"

He waited, and although the wolves were all snarling, not even a single one of them tried to advance.

"What's he doing?" Colton asked. "Has he lost his mind?"

"I don't..."

Clearly at a loss for words, Randall could only stare open-mouthed as Patrick took a step forward, forcing the nearest group of wolves to back further away.

"What's happening?" Colton continued. "Why are they scared of him?"

"Come on," Patrick hissed. "I know one of you has to be dumb enough to try something. I dare you, make your move and find out what I can do with this thing."

He waited, but already some of the wolves were turning and starting to slink away, as if they truly understood that there was nothing more they could do. With each passing second, more and more of the beasts were turning their backs to the scene and hurrying away into the forest. The remaining wolves lingered for a moment longer, still snarling in an increasingly fruitless attempt to project an air of menace, until even these last specimens finally turned and hurried away.

Patrick kept the badge raised, turning slowly to make sure that every last wolf had fled. In truth, he wasn't sure that he dared to ever lower the badge again, but finally he did just that and to his immense relief the wolves continued their retreat. Once the last of the creatures had disappeared into the forest, he turned and saw the other men staring at him with shocked expressions, and then he looked down at the bloodied chunks of bone and meat that were all that remained of Billy's corpse.

"I don't know exactly what I just witnessed," Colton said cautiously, slowly removing his hat, "but I'm sure glad that it worked."

"How did you do that?" Randall asked. "I don't... I can't..."

"We need to take this poor boy's body back with us," Patrick replied, forcing himself to maintain an air of authority even though he was struggling to keep from shaking. "We're not going any further into wolf territory. Not today. Let's collect Billy's remains in a respectful manner and get out of here. I don't know about the rest of you, but I for one would very much like to go home."

CHAPTER TWENTY-ONE

Today...

SOBOLTON'S TOWN HALL STOOD gloomy and empty, with the evening light casting a reduced glow across a meeting room at the rear of the building. Dust was drifting gently through the air, and at the far end of the room – close to an open window – a series of splitting sounds occasionally disturbed the silence.

Finally, slowly, John Tench got to his feet. Naked and in pain, with a few open cuts still glistening across his body, he took a few seconds to try to get his breath back. He tilted his head to either side, trying to straighten out a few twisted muscles, but he knew he didn't have time to fully recover from his latest transformation.

He hadn't remembered the change that had occurred in the forest, perhaps because that entire nightmarish experience had come as such a shock. This time, however, he'd been aware of the entire process, and he'd felt every agonizing crack of pain as his body had shifted. He still wasn't entirely sure how the whole thing worked, but he'd felt as if his bones were re-configuring themselves deep inside his body, and he'd somehow been aware of the sensation of his own face unfolding from beneath some other set of features.

And he remembered walking across the parking lot.

He'd seen the crowd, and he'd been unable to miss the fear on their faces. Every atom of his mind had felt different, as if some greater instinct had taken over, and he'd had to hold back from attacking as soon as he'd spotted Toby's simpering face. In truth, he worried that he *would* have attacked, that he could easily have forgotten all about the task at hand; fortunately Toby had run off and hidden behind some women at the back of the crowd, which in turn had allowed John to keep his anger under control.

Now, naked and with the worst of the pain starting to recede, he looked around the room and realized that he still had to somehow find anything that might mention the location of the bunkers in the forest. He knew there was an entire room with maps displayed on the walls, and he figured that this might be the best place to start, so he started limping across the open space. By the time he reached the doorway on the far side, the last little trace of his limp had already vanished.

Stepping into the deserted foyer, he looked up the staircase. So far, Lisa's plan was working, but he knew that everything depended upon his ability to find the relevant map. He could only hope that the town hall's survey and environmental services department might yield the necessary information, because deep down he knew that there was no back-up idea.

Reaching the top of the staircase, he looked along the two corridors that led off deeper into the building. He could hear occasional cries and yells coming from outside, and those sounds were enough to tell him that the mob in front of the station was getting whipped up into a frenzy. Eventually things were going to spill over into violence, and he knew that Bob wouldn't be able to hold them off for long, so he quickly began to make his way toward the office at the far end of one of the corridors.

"Just hold on a little longer, Bob," he whispered under his breath. "Help's on its way."

***

Leaning out of the doorway, Lisa watched the deserted alley behind the old surgery. She could hear voices yelling in the distance and she knew that the mob in front of the station was becoming more agitated, which meant that time was of the essence. Finally, once she was sure that the coast was clear, she reached a hand back and gestured for Eloise to follow.

"Come on," she whispered. "We need to move."

"Why can't we just wait here?" Eloise asked, taking hold of her hand.

"Because it's not safe," Lisa explained, already leading her along the alley. "It was only ever a short-term option. We need to get to the rendezvous point at the edge of town and hope that John comes through with the location of the bunkers."

"Why are all those people so angry?"

"People like being angry."

"Why?"

"They just do," she continued, reaching the edge of the alley and stopping for a moment to check that the coast was still clear. "People need to feel emotions. Real emotions. And when there's nothing else left, anger's the easiest one for someone to conjure up on their own."

"But why do they do that?"

"These questions are a little above my pay

grade," she admitted as they began to hurry along an empty street. "All I know is that we have to get away from the center of town. There's no -"

Suddenly a figure stepped around the next corner, and Lisa stopped so abruptly that she almost slammed straight into him. She immediately opened her mouth to apologize, but at the last second she recognized him.

"Lisa, hey," Greg said, offering a faint smile. "It's me, from the garage. We -"

"Greg," she replied, trying not to panic. "Long time, no see."

"I was just heading over to see what's going on," he continued. "Apparently a lot of people are gathering at the sheriff's station to demand -"

Before he could finish, he looked down at Eloise and fell silent.

"Greg," Lisa said cautiously, "we used to get on pretty well. You remember that, don't you?"

"I do," he replied. "That was a long time ago, though."

She swallowed hard.

"I remember that night you, me, Tina and Wade got stuck in McGinty's because that storm had hit," he continued, before pausing for a moment. "That's odd, I hadn't thought about Wade in a long time."

"Greg, please don't tell anyone that you saw us," she replied. "I'm begging you, I just need to get

Eloise away from that mob."

"I heard they want to hand her over to the wolves."

"I can't let them do that," she continued, struggling now to hold back tears. "I don't know if you've got any kids of your own, Greg, but please... try to understand."

He looked past her, and after a moment he spotted several people at the far end of the street.

"They might be part of Toby's group," Lisa said, having also noticed them. "Greg, I have a plan that will save the entire town, but I just need a little longer to get everything sorted out. I just need another couple of hours, and then I swear things will start getting back to normal."

"Lisa..."

"I promise!" she hissed, unable to hide a sense of sheer desperation. "I wouldn't lie to you! John Tench and I came up with a plan, and we just need time to put it into action!"

She waited for an answer, and then she pulled Eloise around the corner so that at least they wouldn't be spotted by anyone else.

"Please, Greg."

He stared at her for a moment, before taking a step back. Opening his mouth, he seemed to be on the verge of saying something, but finally he turned and looked toward the far end of the street.

"Over here!" he yelled finally, waving at the

group. "It's Lisa Sondnes! She's got her kid with her!"

"Why did you do that?" Lisa sobbed, clutching Eloise's hand tight as she took another step back. "We'll never be able to outrun them!"

She could already hear footsteps racing along the street, and finally she pulled Eloise back into a shop doorway in a desperate attempt to hide for a few more seconds.

"Where is she?" a man asked breathlessly as he and the others reached Greg.

"That way," Greg replied, pointing toward the old veterinary surgery. "I just saw them both, and they went that way."

"Are you sure?"

"One hundred per cent," Greg said firmly. "Come on, we need to hurry if we want any chance of catching them."

He glanced briefly at Lisa, and then he led the others away in the opposite direction.

Letting out a huge sigh of relief, Lisa realized that at the last moment Greg had come through for her. She waited as the sound of agitated voices receded into the distance, and then she led Eloise out of the doorway and along the street. Glancing over her shoulder, she figured that with any luck the mob would now be at the exact wrong end of town, giving her a clear route to the meeting point she'd arranged with John.

"I liked that man," Eloise said cautiously. "He seemed nice."

"Yeah, he's very nice," Lisa replied, leading her around another corner as she tried to figure out the quickest way to the far end of town. "Come on, we need to keep moving. Hopefully John won't be too much longer."

CHAPTER TWENTY-TWO

Sobolton, USA – 1869...

"WHY?" EMMA SOBBED, TRYING to struggle free as Henning Carson shoved her down onto her knees in the muddy street. "I don't understand what I've done wrong!"

"Perhaps nothing," Father Vacelli said, watching her with a growing sense of unease as Henning kept her firmly in place. "My child, an accusation has been raised and... we must deal with it swiftly, lest it undermines the whole town."

"What accusation?" she cried out. "I'm innocent of any sin you might name!"

She turned to Walter Wade, who was watching from the porch of a nearby building.

"Where is Sheriff Cochrane?" she asked.

"Please, you must wait until he returns. You can't just take the law into your own hands!"

Walter hesitated, as if he was about to say something, and then – with a guilty expression in his eyes – he turned away.

"What's going on here?" Ignacious Huddlestone asked, limping out of the town hall, leaning heavily on his cane. "What are you all doing to this young woman?"

"She has been accused of something heinous!" Octavia Willoughby announced. "Decent people have reason to believe that she is the Walker, a wolf in human form that makes its way among us and spies upon our every move. Such an action is tantamount to heresy and treason, which is why she must be questioned and – where appropriate – punished!"

"The Walker?" Ignacious replied, furrowing his brow. "Why, I have heard of such a thing but -"

"I have nothing to do with the wolves!" Emma shouted, clearly in a state of great panic. "Why are people saying this about me? Who accuses me?"

"I do!" Octavia said firmly, making her way into the middle of the street and stopping in front of her. "I have observed you and I believe it to be so. You are a filthy wolf that has been sent here to spy on the good people of Sobolton, and now you shall be revealed in all your evil!"

"No!" Emma cried. "Please..."

"What can we do?" Blaze Dooley asked, watching from nearby. "Is there some way we can force her to transform before our eyes?"

"I fear not," Octavia continued, "and in truth, the Walker is liable to go to great efforts in an attempt to conceal the truth. Fortunately, I have been told much about their kind over the years, and I know a surefire test that will determine what she is."

Reaching into her pocket, she pulled out a large, slightly rusty knife.

"What are you doing with that?" Emma gasped, immediately trying to pull back, only for Henning and another man to force her to stay on her knees. "What do you mean to do to me?"

"Why do you fear a fair test?" Octavia asked, as more and more people gathered all around to watch. "I do not mean to put you through anything that I myself shall not endure first. It is only fair that I use myself as an example. The Walker is known to be a shifty creature indeed, but humanity is not its natural form. For that reason, it suffers unduly from pain, and it cannot hide this fact."

"That doesn't even make sense!" Emma shouted.

Two men were on their way over, carrying a wooden table that had been borrowed from

McGinty's. They set the table down between Emma and Octavia before hurrying away again.

"I am a good Christian woman," Octavia continued, "and I feel the power of the Lord flowing through me. That is why I am in so many ways the complete opposite to you." She placed her left hand on the table, with the fingers spread out, and then she turned the knife around in her other hand. "I am also a fair woman," she added. "Wolf, you can avoid this fate if you just admit to the truth."

"I'm not a wolf!" Emma sobbed, and now tears were streaming down her face. "I don't know why anyone would accuse me of something so awful!"

"Observe the response of an honest woman to this test," Octavia continued, stony-faced and determined as she set the rusty blade against the index finger of her right hand, just below the joint. "Let this be the standard that the wolf must try to meet."

"What's she doing?" Walter murmured. "I'm not sure I should be letting -"

"Hush," Ignacious said, putting a hand on the side of the man's arm. "This is perhaps necessary."

Emma opened her mouth to beg again for mercy, but in that moment she saw that Octavia was starting to press the knife down. Unable to believe what was happening, Emma could only watch in horror as Octavia began to cut through her own index finger, slicing easily into the flesh before working on the bone. Blood oozed from either size of the wound, yet Octavia offered no cry or scream – not even the slightest hint of discomfort – as she continued her hideous work.

"Why are you doing this?" Emma whimpered. "Please..."

Before she could get another word out, the blade bumped against the table. Glaring into Emma's eyes, Octavia used the knife to push her own finger aside, revealing the bloodied stump that remained.

"She didn't cry out," a woman said in the crowd. "Did you see that? Octavia cut off her own finger and she barely even blinked."

"She has always been a devout woman," a man added. "The Lord must have been with her today."

"And now," Octavia said firmly, still fixing Emma with a determined glare, "it is your turn."

Although she tried again to pull free, Emma was powerless to fight back as a man grabbed her hand and forced it down onto the table with the fingers splayed out.

"No!" Emma hissed. "You can't do this! I've done nothing wrong!"

"When you hear her cries," Octavia snarled, already placing the blade against the younger woman's left index finger, "you shall know that she is without holy guidance, and that she is in fact a wolf."

"I am no wolf!" Emma shouted. "I am only -"

Suddenly she screamed as the blade sliced deep into her finger. Trying frantically to get away, she was held in place by several men and she could do nothing to stop Octavia slowly but surely sawing her index finger away. Sobbing wildly and with tears flooding down her face, Emma looked up at the heavens and tried to beg for help, but she was in such agony that she couldn't even get any words out.

Octavia, meanwhile, was taking her time, sawing with slow determination as she reveled in the cries that – even now – were filling her ears.

"What does this mean?" Walter asked cautiously. "Is she a witch or not?"

"Not a witch," Ignacious replied, "but a wolf most likely. I confess that I had not suspected a thing, but Octavia said it would be thus. And clearly it is."

Still sobbing, Emma was powerless to resist as Octavia finally finished cutting off her finger. The older woman brushed the severed digit onto the ground, and then she watched as blood soaked out from the stump.

"I'm not a wolf!" Emma screamed, as her

whole body shook with a series of unstoppable, violent sobs. "Why won't anyone believe me?"

"The proof is clear!" Octavia shouted, turning to the assembled crowd with the knife still in her right hand. "By any measure, she has failed the one true test. She is a wolf, and she has been spying on us for many years! We have nurtured and fed a beast in our midst, and be thou not uncertain on the matter... that the Lord has seen all, and He shall surely judge our foolishness. Our only hope for salvation comes if we correct our mistake with great alacrity! We must show the Lord that we, a community of foolish sinners, can at least recognize and correct our mistakes before it is too late!"

A cheer erupted from the crowd, and several men hauled the sobbing Emma to her feet. Stepping around her, Octavia pushed a foot down against Emma's severed finger, burying it in the dirt as she made her way closer and looked into the crying woman's face.

"How does it feel, foul creature?" she asked. "Do you feel shame that you have finally been detected? Or does the evil that flows through your veins prohibit such emotion?"

"I'm rather confused," Walter said, wiping sweat from his brow. "What happens now? I'm the deputy and Sheriff Cochrane's away, so should I... should I do something?"

"There is nothing you can possibly do,"

Ignacious replied, with a hint of sadness in his voice as he watched the men dragging Emma away toward the far end of the street. "They know what they mean to do now, and no-one can stop them. We can only pray that they are correct."

CHAPTER TWENTY-THREE

Today...

DEEP BENEATH THE SIDEWALK, the bone of Emma McShane's severed finger lay packed tight in the dirt. For more than a century now, this bone had slowly been driven further and further underground, while people had gone about their lives above, unaware of the events that had transpired many years earlier on this exact spot.

Now, with the afternoon light starting to dim, Lisa Sondnes led her daughter Eloise along the sidewalk, making for the rendezvous point ahead.

"How much further do we have to go?" Eloise asked wearily. "Mommy, I'm so tired."

"It's not far now," Lisa told her. "Come on, just keep walking."

"Are we going back into the forest? I don't want to go into the forest."

"We won't be going far," Lisa explained, constantly looking around for any hint that they might have been spotted. "I don't think so, anyway. Hopefully we won't need to, because I'm pretty sure the wolves have a tight cordon that won't let us get too far from the edge of town. With a little luck, though, we should be absolutely fine."

Reaching the corner, she stepped into the old bus shelter and took another look around. This was the exact spot where she'd arranged to meet John, and she could only hope that he'd be along soon. Most people seemed to have headed into the center of town to either join or observe the disturbance outside the sheriff's station, but Lisa knew full well that danger might yet appear at any moment. She took a seat in the shelter, with Eloise next to her, and already she was starting to fidget uncomfortably as she wondered just what was taking John so long.

She carefully set his clothes on the next seat, ready for his arrival.

"Those people are angry about me," Eloise said cautiously.

Lisa turned to her.

"You always say it's not true," the girl continued, "but it is."

"Sweetheart -"

"I've heard them saying that this is all my fault. Mommy, was it wrong of me to run away from the cabin like that? You told me to do it, but everything has gone wrong since then."

"You did perfectly," Lisa told her. "We had to get away. We couldn't stay there."

"Why not?"

"It's hard to explain."

"Daddy was mad at us both," Eloise pointed out, "but... he wasn't *always* mad. What if we go back? Would everyone in the town be happy then?"

"That's never going to happen," Lisa said firmly.

"But -"

"I have a plan," Lisa continued. "Or part of one, at least. Once we're in the bunker, the wolves should lose your scent and then we'll be able to trick them into thinking that we somehow escaped."

"Do we have to stay in the bunker forever?"

"No, only until they've allowed the town to go back to normal. Then we can sneak out and run before they even have a chance to notice."

"Where will we go?"

"As far away from Sobolton as we can, and we'll never look back."

"But what do the wolves want with me, anyway?" she asked. "Did I do something to upset them?"

"Of course not. It's just... it's very

complicated."

"You keep saying things like that," Eloise replied. "Do you think I'm too young to understand? Or am I just too stupid?"

"You're not stupid," Lisa said firmly. "Never think that. It's just that we're both caught up in something that's much bigger than we can properly understand. We can't reason with the wolves, so we have to get away from them instead. I know it's scary right now, but eventually we'll be able to live without this fear. You just have to trust me for a little while longer, okay?"

She waited for a moment, but Eloise was clearly deep in thought. Finally she pulled the girl closer and kissed the top of her head.

"This is so nearly all over," she continued. "I won't let anything bad happen to you, Eloise. You'll see. Soon all of this will just be a very bad memory."

***

Another cracking sound rang out, then another, and finally the front door of the sheriff's station crumpled, smashing down against the floor and immediately allowing the crowd to start forcing their way inside.

"Find them!" Toby shouted angrily. "They could be hiding anywhere! We've got people covering the sides of the building, so make sure you go through every single room!"

"Are we certain that they're in here?" Zach asked, catching up to him and watching for a moment as other members of the mob fanned out to search the station. "A guy said he saw them heading over toward Lisa's old surgery."

"Oh, they're in here," Toby said firmly, as if he had no doubt whatsoever. "I can feel it in my gut."

"But -"

"Are you gonna stand around yapping," he continued, "or are you actually gonna help? Because the way I see it right now, Zachary, you're not doing much at all to get this situation under control. In fact, part of me wonders whether you're actually some kind of sleeper agent who's been sent to slow us down."

"I'll join the search," Zach replied, turning and hurrying past the reception desk and along toward the sheriff's office.

"See that you do that," Toby sneered, looking around again. "I'm not -"

"We've got one!" a voice yelled, and Toby turned to see several men shoving Robert Law along the corridor. "We found him in one of the offices!"

"Get your filthy hands off me!" Robert snapped, trying to pull free as he limped into the reception area. "You should all be ashamed of yourselves!" he continued, looking around at the figures who'd stopped to watch. In the distance, more people could be heard trashing the building as they continued their search. "Is this all it takes to turn a group of law-abiding citizens into anarchists? How many times are you going to come to this station and shout your demands?"

"Insulting us won't do any good," Toby told him. "That's all you've got, Doctor Law, isn't it? Insults and vile false accusations."

He took a step closer.

"Have you ever stopped to look at things from our point of view, Doctor Law?" he continued. "No, because you've just written us off as a bunch of morons. You probably laugh about us behinds our backs. I bet you call us every name under the sun when we're not listening."

"You're paranoid," Robert replied. "I don't know what's worse. The state of you, or the willingness of these supposedly good people to go along with you."

He turned and looked again at some of the others.

"Tim Carmichael," he continued. "I've known your parents for thirty years. They're good people, they didn't raise you to get involved with something like this."

"We just want our town back," Tim said

cautiously, although he couldn't quite meet Robert's gaze. "We want the wolves to leave us alone."

"By feeding a young girl to them?"

"No-one's feeding anyone to anything," Toby said with a heavy sigh. "Enough with this misinformation, Doctor Law. The wolves aren't savages. The kid belongs to them, she's one of them, so it stands to reason that she should be among her own kind." He took a few more steps closer, until he was right in front of the doctor. "I was there that morning," he continued, "when she was found under the ice. I saw her dead body, and I even helped transport it into your office so that you could perform an autopsy."

"Those facts are not in dispute," Robert replied.

"So I know that she's not right," Toby continued. "That she's not like a regular human. She might be able to pretend that she's one, but she died and came back to life. Call me crazy, but I don't really like people who can do stiff like that, and I sure as hell don't want them in my town. Let's just let her go and take her rightful place with the wolves, and then we can all get back to normal. So tell me, Doctor Law... where is she?"

"You won't find her," Robert said firmly. "She's not -"

Suddenly Toby grabbed him by the shoulder and pulled him down, before slamming a knee into his chest and then shoving him down against the floor.

"That's the wrong answer!" he screamed, as Robert desperately tried to get back up. "How much longer are you gonna lie to us? When are you gonna show up the respect we deserve?"

With that he kicked Robert in the head, then again, before pulling him up and slamming him against the wall and then raining punch after punch onto him as if he'd finally lost all control. And as the others simply watched the onslaught, Robert's unconscious body shuddered time and again while blood began to burst from cuts all over his face.

CHAPTER TWENTY-FOUR

Sobolton, USA – 1869...

"SO WHAT ARE WE gonna tell people?" Randall asked finally, breaking the silence that had persisted for almost the entire ride back to Sobolton. "Billy's parents are gonna want to know what happened to their boy, and everyone's gonna want to know about the wolves."

"We'll tell them the truth," Patrick replied, as he led the posse past the first buildings on the edge of town.

"What if that makes 'em panic?" Randall continued.

"No good ever came of hiding the truth from people," Patrick continued. "The citizens of Sobolton are adults and they deserve to be told what's going on. Besides, you saw what happened out there. As soon as I went near them with the badge, the wolves scattered."

Looking down at the badge, which was now back on the front of his shirt, he again wondered just how a small piece of bone could possibly have had such a huge impact. At the same time, he figured he wasn't exactly smart enough to understand, especially if the whole thing was down to some kind of science.

"We've only got one badge, though," Randall pointed out. "What use is that if someone else heads out into the forest?"

"The wolves know that we have it," Patrick explained. "They know we can use it, too. My hope is that they'll leave us alone now. If they knew about it before, perhaps they needed a little reminder. Either way, my belief is that we won't be troubled by them again, at least not for a long time."

"I hope you're right," Randall murmured.

"So do I," Patrick said as he guided Blackspot around the next corner. "If only -"

Stopping suddenly, he saw that a human figure was hanging limply from a noose attached to a set of makeshift gallows. He could only tell so far that the figure appeared to be a woman, and he watched as several children took turns to pull on the corpse's feet, as if they were trying to drag it down and tighten the rope around its neck.

"Hey, get away from there!" he shouted, forcing Blackspot to set off again. "Go!"

The children turned to look at him, and then they scattered in different directions as Patrick finally reached the spot directly in front of the gallows. He looked up, and in that moment he felt a thud of shock in his chest as he saw the dead, bulging eyes of Emma McShane staring back down at him.

***

"Listen, it wasn't exactly like that," Walter said, holding his hands up in defense as he backed away across the office. "Sheriff, don't be angry with me! I didn't do nothing!"

"You let an innocent woman hang!" Patrick snarled, advancing until Walter was fully back up against the wall.

"There was nothing I could do about it!" the smaller man protested, spraying saliva from his lips in the process. "They were dead set on it, and they seemed to think they were right, and even Mr. Huddlestone didn't think I should get involved!"

Patrick raised a fist.

"Walter's entirely correct," a voice said suddenly.

Turning, Patrick saw Ignacious Huddlestone standing in the doorway.

"I came as soon as I heard you boys were back in town," the old man continued. "Sheriff, a lot has gone down since you headed out a few hours ago. I'm not here to defend it all, but I think you need to at least hear about it properly before you go around accusing people of being fools. Now, there are a lot different parts to this story, so you might need to pay attention properly if you're gonna have any hope of understanding it right."

"Why did you hang Emma?" Patrick asked.

"For centuries -"

"Why did you hang her?" Patrick snapped angrily, briefly closing his hands to form fists. "What the hell is wrong with the people of this town?"

"She was tested," Ignacious explained, "and she failed that test. We all witnessed it."

"That's right," Walter continued. "Everyone saw it. Everyone heard her screaming."

Patrick turned and raised a fist again.

"It was a fair test!" Walter insisted, holding his hands up in a desperate attempt to protect himself. "Ask the priest! I don't remember his name, but go and ask him! He wouldn't have allowed anything to happen if he didn't think it was right! The McShane woman was a witch!"

"Not a witch," Ignacious said, with the tired tone of someone who was sick of correcting an imbecile. "A wolf."

"Get out of here, Walter," Patrick sneered. "Get out before I change my mind and beat you to death."

"I don't see how that's fair," Walter replied, taking care to stay as far away from Patrick as he headed to the door. "You weren't here, you don't know how it was."

"I'll be needing a new deputy," Patrick said firmly. "Don't come back in here, Walter. In fact, you should probably keep out of my sight altogether. If I ever see your damn ugly face again, I'm liable to rearrange it."

He waited until Walter had left the room, and then he slowly turned and looked once more at Ignacious.

"I'm sorry, Patrick," the old man said. "I know you'd taken a liking to Emma. I even had a thought that you and her might be married at some point. She was a good young woman, I must admit that I liked her a great deal and I never suspected that anything was wrong with her."

"What was she accused of?" Patrick asked.

"Octavia Willoughby accused her of being the Walker," Ignacious explained. "That's a wolf that takes human form and walks in the town, spying on us and generally causing trouble."

"Emma was no such thing," Patrick spat back at him. "Even a fool could see that."

"Well, that might be where you're wrong,"

Ignacious insisted. "I admit that I myself was extremely skeptical at the start of it all, but then Octavia got to explaining herself and, as it turned out, she sorta had some decent points. She came up with a way of testing it – a totally fair way, as it happens – and, well, to my great surprise poor Emma was unable to pass that test." He hesitated. "I suppose I shouldn't call her *poor* Emma now, not with what we all know."

Patrick took a step toward him, but Ignacious immediately pulled back as if he was terrified.

"Do you really think I'd strike an old man?" Patrick sneered.

"I get that this is difficult," Ignacious replied, "but you're a lawman. You need to be able to put emotion aside for one moment when you're making a professional judgment. And let's be completely frank with one another for a moment here, Sheriff Cochrane. How many times did you actually meet Emma? Twice? Three times, at most? That's hardly enough for you to get a proper read of her character, is it? Why, you were probably just blinded by her undoubted beauty, that's all. I don't blame you, you're a red-blooded male, you took one look at her and thought she'd make a fine wife. If you want my opinion, you've managed to avoid making a terrible mistake."

"A good woman is hanging out there in the

street," Patrick said darkly, "and *I'm* supposedly the one who made a mistake?"

"Life isn't fair," Ignacious continued, "especially not out here on what I suppose you'd call the frontier. Chalk this up to experience and use it to inform your future decisions. Meanwhile, once things have settled I'll personally help you pick yourself a wife. There are some lovely unmarried ladies in the town and some of them come from quite good families. Tell me, how much importance do you attach to the state of a woman's teeth?"

Patrick hesitated, before turning and walking back over to the doorway.

"That's right," Ignacious called after him. "Just go somewhere and cool down for a little while, and then I'm sure you'll feel so much better! Everything's still raw, isn't it? Like I said, emotions can be quite overwhelming and we all have to learn to conquer them from time to time. One day you'll look back on today and realize that this is the moment when you truly began to fit in as part of our little town. In fact, I wouldn't mind betting that one day you'll even look back on it all and manage a chuckle!"

He waited, but Patrick was gone. Left standing alone, Ignacious let out a heavy sigh.

"People just have to realize how things work around here, that's all," he continued, sounding slightly melancholic now. "You can't just storm in and change it all. Sometimes you've gotta work with what you find."

CHAPTER TWENTY-FIVE

Today...

STANDING NAKED IN ONE of the town hall's many meeting rooms, John continued to pore over various documents that he'd found in one of the cabinets. He was far from an experienced map reader, especially when it came to technical maps used by various departments, but one particular map showed the forest around Sobolton and appeared to mark half a dozen specific sites.

As he peered more closely at the map, John realized that the sites seemed to be linked to various measurements referring to depth and volume. Although he couldn't be certain, this was the only map that might possibly relate to the supposed bunkers in the forest, and finally he realized that his search was at an end. He rolled the map up and secured it with an elastic band, and then he hurried out of the room and made his way down the main staircase.

Already, he was starting to wonder exactly how he was going to get back across town and find Lisa, although deep down he knew that there was only one answer. He was going to have to transform into a wolf again, despite all the pain that went with such a change, although he also figured that he might be able to remain in his human form and go through some of the back streets and alleyways.

Reaching the bottom of the staircase, he was already starting to favor the latter idea. He headed around the corner, intending to go out through the back door, but in that moment a figure stepped around from the other side and almost slammed straight into him.

Pulling back, John was shocked to find himself face to face with Zach from the office.

"Sheriff Tench?" Zach stammered, before looking him up and down for a moment. "What... what are you doing here?"

"What are *you* doing here?" John asked as he desperately tried to figure out how he was going to escape.

"I was sent to look for..."

Zach's voice trailed off for a few seconds.

"You," he added finally.

"By Toby?"

Zach hesitated, and then he nodded.

"Actually, he didn't send me," Zach explained. "Not technically. It's just that things are getting heated over at the station and I wanted to get away, so I thought I'd come to the town hall and try to be useful and..."

His voice trailed off again.

"Well, I'm here," John continued, setting the rolled-up map on a nearby table for a moment.

"You sure are," Zach replied, before looking him up and down again. "And you're..."

John waited for him to finish.

"Sir," Zach said cautiously, "I don't mean to be rude or anything, but... why are you naked?"

"That's an excellent question," John replied. "A truly *outstanding* question. And the thing is, I don't really have an answer that I care to give you right now."

"Are you taking something from the town hall?" Zach asked, looking at the map on the table. "Are you... burglarizing the town hall... while you're naked?"

"I guess it sure looks like that," John

replied. "Let me ask you something, though. Are you here alone?"

"Me?"

Zach paused for a few seconds, before nodding.

"Yes, Sir," he continued, furrowing his brow. "I am. Why?"

***

Ten seconds later, Zach slumped down unconscious onto the floor. Stepping around him, John took hold of his hands and began to drag him through into the next room, which turned out to be the entrance to the town's museum.

"Sorry, Zach," he muttered under his breath, setting the man down next to a display cabinet, "but right now I have to do what I have to do. And you could always have picked the right side in this mess."

Taking a step back, he briefly wondered whether he could strip Zach down and borrow his uniform, although he quickly realized that the guy was too short. Sighing, and slightly annoyed that such an easy solution had slipped away, he turned and looked around – and at that moment he once again saw one of the mannequins at the far end of the room, dressed in a period outfit.

Making his way over, John peered at the description on the wall.

"Actual sheriff's uniform," he whispered as he read, "worn around the turn of the century in Sobolton."

He looked at the uniform again, and saw that it seemed to be in good condition and that – crucially – it appeared to be approximately his size. He tried to open the cabinet, only to find that it was locked, but he figured that shouldn't be too much of a problem, especially since a handy fire extinguisher was standing nearby. As he looked at a second cabinet, however, he realized that another old uniform was on display, along with some dusty shoes and various other items that would have been worn by people back in the day.

"Well," he said finally, spotting his own naked figure reflected dimly in the glass, "I can't go out there like this, can I?"

Taking the fire extinguisher, he held it up and prepared to strike. When he made his move, the glass of the first cabinet shattered instantly, so he did the same to the next section before discarding the extinguisher and starting to carefully remove the old uniform from the mannequin. The fabric was rough and dry, and slightly worn in place, but for the most part the uniform seemed to be in surprisingly good condition. As he began to slip into his new clothes, John couldn't help but admire the irony that he was about to get dressed up as a good old-fashioned lawman. He even spotted a hat on a display stand, although he knew that would be a step too far.

After slipping into the boots, which also fit surprisingly well, he made his way over to a nearby door and tried to check out his own reflection in the glass.

For a few seconds, he could only stare at the bizarre sight. Sure, the uniform was old; there was no getting around that fact. At the same time, it wasn't *too* old or unusual, and he was relieved to realize that he looked vaguely respectable rather than – as he'd feared – freakishly cartoonish. He took a moment to brush the shirt down, and in the back of his mind he was starting to think that there was actually something to be said for the old-fashioned styles.

"Okay," he said, turning and heading past the broken cabinets. "Let's -"

Stopping suddenly, he saw some more old items in the nearest cabinet. Although he knew he was in a hurry, he couldn't help but lean into one of the broken sections, and he saw a crusty old belt as well as some antique guns that had clearly seen better days. The guns couldn't possibly fire, he knew that, and he figured that the old metal spurs would jangle way too loud if he tried to fix them to his boots. Finally he reached in and took the belt; he didn't actually need a belt in that moment, but something about the old leather made him feel nostalgic for a past he'd never even known. Reaching down, he began to thread the belt through the old loops in his 'borrowed' trousers. He knew he was mixing and matching from different historical periods now, but he didn't much care about that. All he knew was that he felt surprisingly comfortable.

"Look complete," he murmured, before heading back across the room. "Sorry again, Zach," he added, stepping over the unconscious man. "When you wake up and this is all over, let's just pretend that the whole naked encounter never happened."

Once he'd picked up the map again, he headed to the rear of the building and peered outside. He'd half expected to hear howls and screams from the crowd outside the station, although in actual fact he heard only the occasional yell. The mob, while considerable, clearly hadn't unleashed full-on violence, at least not yet. For that, he felt grateful as he carefully climbed back out and dropped down into the alley.

As soon as he reached the corner, he saw that the mob had managed to get into the station. He felt a flicker of concern for Bob, but he told himself that the doctor would be able to handle himself; meanwhile the mob would very soon find out that Eloise was nowhere to be found, which meant that they'd become more focused in their efforts to search for her in the town. And that, in turn, made his mission far more urgent.

Heading the other way, he set off through the night, trying to figure out the easiest route that would get him to the rendezvous point. After that, he was going to study the map a little more closely and then lead Lisa and Eloise to the nearest bunker. And then, with a little luck, their harebrained scheme to trick the wolves might actually get a chance to work.

CHAPTER TWENTY-SIX

Sobolton, USA – 1869...

"SO THAT WAS REALLY my thinking on the matter," Walter said, as he sat on a stool outside the ramshackle little bar on the town's main street. "I mean, how long have I been here? Not long enough to start interfering, that's for sure. And I don't think I actually did anything wrong, so it's not fair to put all the blame on me when I'm not the one who strung her up there."

He looked along the street and saw Emma McShane's corpse still hanging in the distance. The sight sent a shiver through his bones, but his sense of indignation returned and he quickly took another swig of beer.

"That's been the story of my life, though,"

he continued. "People have always been quick to blame me for things that weren't my fault. The Great Dafford Mine Collapse of 1860. The Westerham Mill Explosion of 1862. The Second Great Dafford Mine Collapse of 1865. And I've never really stood up for myself because, well, I don't like starting a fight unless I really have to. So I guess you could say that my problem is I'm just too nice, and too kind. I'm always -"

"There he is," murmured Owen McGinty, the bar's proprietor, as he saw Patrick emerging from one of the nearby buildings. "Sure looks to me like our sheriff's in a bad mood."

"Do you think I should go over to him?" Walter asked.

After waiting for an answer, he turned to Owen.

"Well? Do you?"

"I'm sorry, I haven't really been listening," Owen said with a sigh. "You're your own man, do as you please. All I really care about is that you've got enough to pay for that beer." He turned and glared at him. "You *have* got enough to pay for it, right?"

"You'll get your money," Walter replied as he saw Patrick heading toward the wooden church at the far end of the next street. "Now, why do you suppose he's going in there?"

"Now you're not a deputy," Owen

continued, "shouldn't you be getting on with finding a job?"

"Don't worry about me," Walter said, keeping his eyes very much fixed on Patrick, watching as the sheriff stepped inside the church and disappeared from view. "I'll pay you, alright."

He took another, longer swig of beer.

"I need a wife," he continued, sounding pretty sorry for himself now. "That's what I'm after, someone who'll help me look smart. Someone who'll feed me right. With a wife by my side, I'll be a much better man."

"If you're in need of a wife," Owen replied, "then Marion Doggett over there's been searching for a husband for a while now. She arrived not long ago from England and, well, she's been pursuing a number of suitors without much luck. The thing about Marion is, once she sniffs a chance with a man, she latches on and won't let go. Poor Ralph Hyde had to die to get away from her. She's tenacious and she knows what she wants. She's certainly been determined since she got here, but also a little unlucky."

"She has, huh?" Walter said, turning to see a pretty woman washing some clothes in a tin bath nearby. Sitting up straighter, he began to brush mud from his shirt. "She looks just my type, too."

As if she'd sensed that she was being watched, Marion turned and looked at him. Walter offered a crooked smile, and in return Marion smiled back, revealing three yellowish-black teeth set into rotten and bloodily-swollen gums.

***

"Octavia Willoughby," Patrick said, stopping in the church's central aisle and looking at the woman as she remained on her knees before the altar. "I'll be having a word with you now about what happened while I was away."

He waited, but she showed no sign that she'd even heard him.

"Octavia Willoughby," he continued, "there's a good woman hanging from a post outside, and I've been told that you were instrumental in sealing her fate. If you've used lies and deception to get a woman killed, that's of interest to me."

"I used no lies and no deception," she replied archly, still not turning to him. "I was guided by the Lord in all things."

"Emma McShane was no wolf."

"How can you know that for sure?"

"Because I have eyes."

"But how can you know that she did not transform?" she asked. "You think too simply. These beasts are capable of changing their forms to suit the environment. They present themselves in ways that please the eyes of those they mean to control. I'm sure it did not escape your notice that Emma was easy to look at."

"I'm talking about her soul," he replied, still just about managing to contain his anger. "She was a good, honest citizen, yet you've evidently made her out to be a woman of secrets."

"We're going around in circles with this conversation," she replied, slowly getting to her feet and finally turning to him. "She was given the opportunity to prove herself, and she failed that test."

Holding up her hand, she revealed the bloodied stump that she still had not covered with any kind of bandage.

"I took the test myself, to prove that it could be done."

"I'm not sure that I trust anyone who would willingly cut off one of her own fingers," he pointed out.

"But I did it in service of the Lord," she replied, "and in service of this great town. I did it to prove that if the Lord is within one's soul, one *can* withstand such pain." She paused, almost smiling as she studied the expression on his face. "You should have heard her cries, Sheriff Cochrane," she continued finally. "You should have heard how she begged for her life, and how she screamed in sheer agony. There could be no doubt, she was utterly abandoned by the Lord in her final moments. Why do you think that should be the case, unless she was the very thing I accused her of being?"

"You're out of your mind," he sneered.

"Granted, I had a little experience in such matters," she said, before reaching up and starting to unbutton her shirt. "I have always tested myself, and I always shall."

Before Patrick could reply, Octavia pulled her shirt aside, revealing a pair of heavy-hanging breasts with cuts and marks and scars all over them. A moment later she pulled the shirt off altogether, showing that her arms too had clearly been sliced and gouged many times over the years.

"Every inch of my body is covered," she purred happily, "and I have never once cried out. I work at night, mostly, cutting into my own flesh, going as deep as I dare and then deeper still. Sometimes I even feel the tip of my knife grinding against bone, but I don't let that stop me. I carve messages, mostly, and warnings to the Devil. I pride myself on smiling as I work, to prove to myself that the Lord is with me. Yet pretty, young Emma McShane was unable to keep her mouth shut for so much as one second when I took something as insignificant as a solitary finger."

"She was no wolf," he snarled, disgusted by the sight before him.

"You'll see," she continued, as tears of joy filled her eyes. "You'll all see eventually that I was right. She was the Walker and as such she was a scourge upon our town, so she had to be -"

Suddenly Patrick pulled his pistol from its holster and held it up, aiming at her face.

"Do it," she said firmly, and now her smile grew broader still. "Cut me down, and the Lord will welcome me into his kingdom as his most humble servant. I have been waiting for such a day. Then all in this town shall see that I was right from beginning to end."

With his finger pressing against the trigger, Patrick felt an overwhelming urge to end Octavia's life. He wanted to blow her head clean open, but at the last second he held back as he felt a niggling concern moving to the front of his mind. He'd noticed something earlier, something that he'd barely even thought about, yet now that observation seemed too huge to ignore. Realizing that he might have been an utter fool, he lowered the gun and turned, heading out of the church.

"Will you not do it today, Sheriff?" Octavia called after him. "Will you not send me on my way to eternal glory? I was so sure that you were about to do it. Please, why do you not come back now and do for me the one thing I cannot do for myself?"

"I won't give you the satisfaction," he sneered as he headed out through the main door. "Enjoy the rest of your miserable life. I hope it's long."

CHAPTER TWENTY-SEVEN

Today...

"SHE'S NOT HERE!" A voice cried out at the far end of the corridor, followed by the sound of something heavy crashing against the floor and then glass shattering. "We've checked everywhere! There's no sign of her!"

"Then spread out!" Toby yelled, storming across the station's reception area and picking his way out through the broken door. "We know they can't have gone far, so fan out in groups and search everywhere. This whole thing was a decoy. I won't be made to look like a fool! Hurry!"

As more voices shouted at each other, a faint groaning sound could be heard outside the door to John Tench's office. A few seconds later, having finally stirred, Robert Law somehow managed to sit up. Beaten and bloodied, with a heavy cut on his split left cheek and swelling around one eye, he shifted around and leaned back against the wall. Every breath was agony as fractured ribs cut through his body, and he knew he had to stay focused if he was to stand any chance of remaining conscious. He'd already passed out once, and as he looked along the corridor he saw that the entire station had been completely trashed.

Suddenly hearing footsteps, he turned to see a figure hurrying over. He immediately began to pull away, terrified that he was about to suffer another beating.

"It's me," Cassie stammered, dropping to her knees. "Doctor Law, what did they do to you?"

Turning again, he saw that she too was hurt, with cuts all over one side of her face and a thick split lip. She reached out and touched his shoulder, and although he instinctively shuddered and tried to get away, he managed to force himself to stay calm.

"Doctor Law," she continued, "can you hear me?"

He began to nod, and this too brought more pain.

"They've really done a number on you," she continued, and now tears were filling her eyes. "Hold tight and I'll call for help."

"Can't," he stammered.

"Damn it, you're right," she said. "The phones are still down. Okay, then... I'll find someone."

Very slowly, despite the agony, he shook his head.

"You're really very badly hurt," she told him.

"So... are you," he whispered.

"Me? I've had worse." She leaned closer and looked at the large bloodied split on his cheek. "These aren't just cuts and bruises," she continued. "You need proper medical help. I think... I'm going to have to take you to the Overflow."

"I don't... have time for... hospital now," he murmured.

"You don't have any choice," she said, before reaching around him and starting to help him up. "Can you stand? Hopefully at least one of the patrol cars out the back is still fit to drive, otherwise we've got a long walk ahead of us."

"Where... did they go?" he asked, limping heavily as she helped him along the corridor. "Toby and his goons, I mean. Where are they searching next?"

"Everywhere, I think," she replied, helping him out onto the steps at the front of the station. "I don't know where Sheriff Tench took Lisa and the girl, but I sure hope they've found a good place to hide."

"They won't be hiding," Robert explained through gritted teeth. "That's not John Tench's way. He'll have a plan, and he'll be getting on with it. And if I know that man at all... he'll find a way to stop this madness and save the town."

***

"Mommy, I'm cold," Eloise said as she and Lisa sat at the bus stop on McShane Street, still waiting for John to arrive. "It's getting dark. Are we going to have to sit here much longer?"

"I hope not," Lisa replied, leaning forward and looking both ways but still seeing no sign of John. "Just hold tight, okay?" She reached out toward her daughter and pulled her close for a hug. "Come here, we can keep each other warm."

"I wish this wasn't all my fault," Eloise replied, shuffling along the bench and leaning in for the embrace. "I wish people weren't angry and unhappy because of me."

"It's not because of you," Lisa said firmly. "I've told you before, you mustn't think like that. Yes, people are scared and angry, but you're not responsible for how they react to things. That applies as much to the humans as it does to the wolves." She kissed the top of Eloise's head and breathed deep, taking in her daughter's scent. "You're the most special little girl in the whole world, but it's not fair that people are fighting over you like this. That's why we have to get as far away from them as possible."

"But -"

"And there's really no other possibility," Lisa continued. "You're too young to understand it all right now."

"Why am I too young?"

"You just are."

"But why?"

"Because it's complicated."

Eloise sat in silence for a moment, struggling to work out exactly what her mother meant.

"I still feel like it's my fault," she whimpered finally, "and -"

Suddenly voices called out in the distance. Lisa got to her feet and looked along the street, and sure enough she spotted three figures making their way closer. In a split second she pulled Eloise out of the shelter and around the side, and she quickly put a finger to her lips, reminding her daughter to stay quiet as the men approached.

"It's like looking for a needle in a haystack," one of them was complaining, as they reached the bus stop and Lisa silently pulled Eloise around to the rear. "Hell, it's worse than that. At least if you're looking for a needle in a haystack, eventually you're gonna feel a little prick to tell you you've found it."

"You'd know all about little pricks," one of the other men laughed.

"Again with the dumb jokes," the first guy said with a sigh. "Don't you ever get tired of just being relentlessly unfunny?"

Not even daring to breathe, Lisa heard the three men fall silent. She tried to focus on the sound of their footsteps getting further and further away, although after a few seconds she realized that she couldn't actually hear anything at all. She wasn't sure whether they'd gone or whether they'd stopped on the other side of the bus stop, so she simply stood silently listening for any kind of clue.

All she heard, however, was the rustling of nearby trees as a breeze blew past.

Looking down at Eloise, she saw the fear in the girl's eyes. She desperately wanted to tell her that everything was going to be alright, and that John would be along at any moment, but deep down she knew that her so-called plan was hanging by a thread and that they were going to need a huge amount of luck. She felt as if she should have been better at protecting her daughter, and she promised herself in that moment that as soon as they got away from Sobolton everything was going to be better. Eloise was going to live a normal life and -

"Got you!"

Suddenly two hands grabbed her and pulled her back, and a second man took Eloise's arm and yanked her away.

"No!" Lisa shouted, trying in vain to break free as the man turned her around and slammed her against the back of the bus stop. "You can't do this! She's just a child!"

"Mommy, help!" Eloise gasped as the two others began to pull her around to the side of the road.

"You shouldn't have run," the first man sneered, spraying Lisa's ear with spittle as he leaned closer to the side of her face. Already, Eloise could be heard struggling frantically nearby. "You realize that, right? This could all have been avoided if you'd just been smart and thought about other people for a change."

"Get off me!" she snarled, trying to twist free. "I swear, if you hurt her I'll -"

"You'll *what*?" the man asked, leaning even closer now, filling her nostrils with the stench of his rotten breath. "What's the poor little mommy gonna do to protect her daughter, huh? You got any special abilities you wanna break out and use, Lisa Sondnes? Are you secretly a boxer or a ninja? No? I didn't think so."

"Eloise, don't be scared!" Lisa shouted. "Everything's going to be okay!"

"For the rest of us, sure," the man said firmly. "But Toby only told us to get the kid, so I guess that means we don't need you."

"Eloise, just -"

"Nighty night!" the man added, before slamming Lisa's head against the back of the shelter, knocking her out instantly and leaving her unconscious body to slither down onto the grass.

CHAPTER TWENTY-EIGHT

Sobolton, USA – 1869...

"AH, SHERIFF COCHRANE," IGNACIOUS Huddlestone said as he continued to make some notes at his desk. "I thought it might be a little longer before I received a visit from you, but -"

"How could you do it?" Patrick asked, stopping in the middle of the room.

Ignacious looked up at him.

"How could you let an innocent woman go to her death," Patrick continued, "for the one crime of which you yourself are guilty?"

"I'm not sure that I follow," Ignacious replied cautiously. "You seem a little agitated. Would you care for a drink?"

Getting to his feet, he shuffled over to a

cabinet on the far side of the office and began to pour two glasses of whiskey.

"I obtained this bottle from some people who passed through the town last winter," he explained. "At first it wasn't very palatable, but as the temperature improved, so too did the whiskey. I'm afraid that I'm not enough of a connoisseur to explain how that works, but the effect is most striking." Once he was done, he turned around and smiled, while holding two filled glasses. "I don't advertise the fact that I have it, because then every man would be at my door begging for some. But you'll try it with me now, will you not?"

"You're the Walker," Patrick replied.

"What could possibly give you that idea?"

"When the men and I returned earlier," he continued, "people asked us what happened out there. They were frantic with worry, they were begging us to make them feel better. It was fear that drove them, and we did our best to console them while also not lying. But you, Mr. Huddlestone, seemed entirely unconcerned about the situation, which I can only assume means that you were already well aware. Perhaps not of the details, but certainly of the overall scope."

"That's an interesting conjecture," Ignacious suggested.

"And there's another thing," Patrick added. "Ever since Emma gave me something to put in this badge, you've conspicuously kept your distance from me. You've come closer, but not close enough for anything to be revealed about you."

"I'm sure I don't know what you're talking about."

"I'll take your whiskey," Patrick told him, before holding out a hand. "Would you mind bringing it over?"

"I'll just set it down here," Ignacious replied, placing one of the glasses on a table and then taking several steps back. "There. It's all yours."

"This item in the badge was almost lost," Patrick continued. "Emma herself told me that it was in the church. You couldn't pick it up and dispose of it yourself, for obvious reasons, but you were able to slowly engineer a situation in which it became almost forgotten. Had it not been for Emma, it might have been lost forever by now, but she still had faith in the old stories. Most of the other people here have forgotten those stories, or they've twisted them for their own purposes, but Emma stuck to what they truly meant. That's why she was so dangerous to you."

"I didn't have her killed," Ignacious pointed out. "I didn't string her up there or administer a test or -"

"But you watched it all happen," Patrick said, interrupting him, "and I'm sure you added a little word of encouragement here and there. Not just today, but over many years."

"Now you're being fanciful," Ignacious chuckled. "I -"

Suddenly Patrick took several strong steps forward, causing his boots to stamp hard against the wooden floor. He quickly walked past the table and the whiskey, and Ignacious couldn't help but pull back around to the other side of the desk.

"Scared of something?" Patrick asked, stopping in front of the desk.

"I'm starting to wonder," Ignacious replied, clearly flustered, "whether I was right to hire you as Sobolton's first sheriff. I'm seeing now that you might not have the proper temperament."

"Is that so?" Patrick murmured, before starting to slowly lean over the desk, moving very slowly closer to the other man. "Or is it actually the case that you simply never anticipated that Emma would try to help me? Did you never realize that she had removed the little piece of bone from the church?"

Ignacious opened his mouth to reply, but at that moment he heard a faint rattling sound. Looking at the badge on Patrick's chest, he saw that it was shaking slightly and that something inside seemed to be banging repeatedly against the metal.

"I can see it in your eyes now," Patrick told him. "Once you see something like this, it's impossible to miss again. It's hard to understand how I ever missed it, but I suppose you're good at hiding the truth. I didn't notice at the time, but you always wore gloves when you handled the badge. How long have you been the Walker, Mr. Huddlestone? I'm thinking it must have been decades and decades, and all the while you've been slowly building yourself up into a position of authority."

"I don't like these accusations," Ignacious replied, unable to hide his anger now as he stepped back against the wall, causing the badge on Patrick's chest to stop rattling. "I don't like what you're trying to suggest."

"How often do you go out to the forest and communicate with your pack?" Patrick asked. "Weekly? Monthly? Or do you only bother when there's something worth telling them?" He looked him up and down. "You're not exactly an impressive-looking specimen, Ignacious. Is that deliberate? Have you intentionally allowed yourself to become old and fat, so that you don't look too threatening?"

Opening his mouth, Ignacious seemed poised to respond, but instead he merely gritted his teeth.

"And how have you kept the deception up for so long," Patrick continued, leaning a little further across the desk, causing the badge to shake and rattle harder than ever, "without -"

Suddenly letting out a roar of anger, Ignacious pushed the desk forward and tipped it over, slamming it against Patrick with immense force and sending the sheriff crashing against the far wall, with the desk thudding into him with such power that he let out a pained gasp.

"You need to stop poking your nose into matters that don't concern you!" the older man shouted angrily, as a hint of yellow and red began to fill his eyes. "Believe it or not, I actually want the best for both worlds! I want your people and mine to share this land, but you humans won't ever agree to that, will you?"

He stepped closer, watching as Patrick – clearly in pain – pushed the desk aside and tried to get to his feet.

"No, you want it all," Ignacious continued. "I've seen enough to know that you're a species defined by lust and greed. You take chunks of the forest, but you're never satisfied so you always take more and more and more! You dig in the ground and take what you find there too, and soon you'll find a way to steal the very air that we breathe! Now there's a railroad coming, it's going to cut straight through the cemetery but nobody cares about that, not really, because they just want new ways to take everything from us! For that matter, one day you'll probably find a way to steal the sun and the moon and the stars from us!"

"We can live in peace," Patrick gasped, "but *this* isn't the way to achieve that!"

"It'll never end. I've tried to stop it, or even to slow it down, but you humans are determined to start a war. And the worst part is, with your endless invention of new machines and new ways of killing, we don't really stand a chance. That's why we have to hide ourselves away and use our few advantages so carefully! My people have a kind of collective memory, Sheriff Cochrane. A folk memory. We know that we have been cursed ever since the day your kind first set foot on this land. We know that we became these half human, half wolf monsters on that day when the gods struck down two warriors on the shore. We know that for hundreds and hundreds of years, you've been driving us further away from our old territory. What are we supposed to do about that? Do you want us to just lie down and die?"

Reaching for his pistol, Patrick managed to pull it from the holster, only to fumble and drop it at the last second. As he tried to pick it up again, Ignacious kicked it away and reached down, grabbing him by the lapels and hauling him up. With eyes that now bulged from their sockets, as if he'd lost control of his transformation, the old man glared at Patrick with undisguised fury as the badge on the sheriff's chest shook furiously.

"Well," Ignacious snarled, "if it's war you pathetic creatures want, then perhaps it's war you should get. And even if the wolves don't win, we'll certainly make sure that you all pay a dear price. If we die, then you'll die too!"

Before Patrick could get a word out, Ignacious let out another roar and threw him across the room. Slamming into the door, which broke under the force of the impact, Patrick tumbled out down the steps and landed in a gasping heap on the dirt, as shocked onlookers up and down the street turned in horror to see what was happening.

Desperately trying to get his breath back, Patrick looked up just in time to see Ignacious – whose wolf form was becoming more and more visible in his features with each passing second – stepped out into the dying evening light.

CHAPTER TWENTY-NINE

Today...

"IS HE..."

Standing in the hospital corridor, Tracy felt for a moment as if she couldn't quite bring herself to complete that question. She'd been waiting for what had seemed like an eternity, listening to voices shouting in the room, but suddenly silence had fallen and she couldn't help but interpret that as the worst possible news.

"My husband," she continued, "is -"

"We've managed to stabilize him again," Nurse Simpson explained. "I'm not going to lie to you, it wasn't easy. We still need to monitor him constantly, to make sure that he doesn't suffer another seizure."

"Seizure?" Tracy replied, furrowing her brow. "Why is he having seizures?"

"That's the million dollar question," the nurse replied. "In ordinary circumstances, we'd have specialists involved and we could send him down for scans, but with things as they are..."

Her voice trailed off for a moment.

"We're doing the absolute best that we can," she added, placing a hand on the side of Tracy's arm. "I hope you realize that."

"Can I see him?"

The nurse hesitated, as if she wasn't quite sure how to answer.

"I want to see my husband," Tracy said firmly.

"Sure, that's fine. That's totally understandable. It's just... you need to know that he's talking, and what he's saying isn't making a great deal of sense."

"What's he talking *about*?" Tracy asked.

"That's just it, we can't really figure it out," the nurse told her. "The best we can tell, it's some kind of gibberish."

"I still want to see him," Tracy replied, pushing past her and entering the room, then making straight for the side of the bed. "Tommy, I'm here," she continued, looking down and seeing that at least he seemed a little calmer now. Taking hold of his hand, she squeezed it tight. "I'm right here and I'm not going anywhere."

Tommy's lips moved, and he murmured something that she wasn't quite able to pick out.

"What was that?" she asked, leaning closer. "Tommy, I didn't hear what you said."

"A thousand years and more," Tommy whispered. "That's how long it has been since that man saw the first of their kind. His name... his name was Ragnar, I think. Yes, definitely Ragnar. He was about to leave this land forever, but first he went to see what had become of his fallen comrade, and what he witnessed..."

He fell silent again.

"I don't know what you're talking about," Tracy told him, as tears once again began to fill her eyes. "Tommy, you're not making any sense at all. Who's Ragnar? What are you trying to tell me?"

***

"Rip it apart!" Toby yelled, as crashing sounds could be heard coming from the window of John's kitchen. "I don't want anything left unturned!"

"Do you really think they'd be here?" one of the other deputies asked. "What -"

"I don't give a damn if they're here or not," Toby continued, his voice echoing out across the street as night continued to slowly fall. "I want to send a message. John Tench isn't welcome here, not anymore. He had a chance to show us that he was on our side and he blew it. Now we're doing things our way. The Sobolton way."

Having stopped for a moment at the end of the road, John listened to the sound of his home being ransacked. He'd expected nothing less, although he was a little surprised that Toby was seemingly overseeing the entire operation. In truth, he would have expected Toby to be out there leading the charge elsewhere, barking orders to his little army, but now he realized that the revolt was becoming extremely personal. He'd long understood that several people in the department resented the way he'd been parachuted into the sheriff's role from out of town, and now he realized that the bitterness and anger ran so very deep.

"Destroy it all!" Toby shouted. "Come on, we haven't got all night! Destroy every damn thing you find!"

Figuring that there was no point lingering, John began to make his way along the street with the map still in his right hand. He knew he was taking a little extra risk by walking straight past his own home, but at the same time he figured that he was far enough away to avoid being seen. Sure enough, as he reached the end of the street, he realized to his relief that he hadn't been spotted, so he continued to pick his way through the town as he tried to get to the rendezvous point.

Suddenly hearing more voices nearby, he ducked back into a doorway. Sure enough, half a dozen men hurried past, chattering excitedly but missing him as they made their way around another corner.

Relieved to have had such a lucky escape, John set off again. He wasn't quite sure what he was going to do if he suddenly ran into part of the mob, but he figured that he'd cross that bridge when he got to it. And then, after a few more minutes, he finally reached the edge of town and saw the bus stop up ahead. He quickened his pace, glancing all around, but when he got to the bus stop he saw to his surprise that there was no sign of Lisa. His clothes, however, had been neatly folded and placed on one of the seats.

"Are you here?" he hissed, worried that she and Eloise might have been caught already. "Lisa, can you hear me?"

He waited, but he heard no hint of a reply.

"Lisa, I've got the map," he continued, turning to look around, hoping against hope that she was merely hiding somewhere nearby. "Lisa, I -"

Before he could finish, he spotted a dark patch on the ground, resting in the grass nearby. Puzzled, he stepped around the bus stop and looked down, and to his surprise he found himself staring at three men who appeared to have been knocked to the ground. Heading over, he reached down and found that they had pulses; they were still alive, although they each cuts on their heads as if they'd been subjected to some kind of blunt trauma.

Stepping back, John turned to look along the street, but a moment later he heard a faint groaning sound coming from nearby.

Spotting movement behind the bus stop, he walked over just as Lisa began to sit up.

"Are you okay?" he asked, crouching down next to her. "Lisa, what happened?"

"I don't..."

Reaching up, she touched the front of her head and winced.

"I don't remember," she whispered. "Wait... three men found us and -"

Suddenly she looked around, before stumbling to her feet.

"Eloise?" she gasped, and then she spotted the unconscious men on the ground. Racing over, she looked down at them for a moment as if she couldn't quite believe what she was seeing.

"Where is she?" John asked. "I think I found the map we were after, but... where's Eloise?"

"They grabbed her," Lisa murmured, clearly still struggling a little to remember everything. "She was talking about how guilty she felt, and then these three men found us and... one of them said they didn't need me, so I think he knocked me out and then..."

She looked around, and then she glanced down at the men on the ground again.

"Who knocked *them* out?" John asked.

"I don't know," she replied, "but there was no-one else here. Just me and her."

"There's not much sign of a disturbance," John pointed out. "I don't think there can have been much of a fight."

"Look!" she hissed, hurrying across the grass before stopping at the edge of the forest, where a solitary set of small footsteps could be seen heading up the dirty slope and away between the trees.

"That's only one pair of tracks," John replied. "It doesn't seem like anyone was with her."

"She must have knocked those buffoons out," Lisa told him, still staring into the forest but seeing no sign of her daughter. After a moment she cupped her hands around her mouth. "Eloise!" she shouted. "Where are you? It's safe now! You can come back!"

"There's no way she could have knocked out three guys," John said cautiously. "Is there? I know she's only partly human. Is it possible that her wolf side would give her that much strength?"

"She's gone to them," Lisa replied, watching the forest for a moment longer before turning to him with panic in her eyes. "John, don't you see what happened here? She told me she feels guilty about what's happening to Sobolton, and I think she finally decided that there's only one way to set things straight." She paused for a few more seconds, as if she couldn't quite get the words out. "She's gone to find them," she added finally. "Eloise has gone to turn herself over to the wolves. She thinks that if she does that, she can save the whole town."

CHAPTER THIRTY

Sobolton, USA – 1869...

"WHAT... WHAT HAPPENED TO him?" a woman asked, stepping back as she saw the horrific sight of Ignacious standing outside the town hall. "What happened to his face?"

Still gasping in pain, Patrick began to sit up. He instinctively reached for his gun, only to find that it was gone.

"Sheriff!"

He turned just in time to see Walter racing over.

"Give me your gun," Patrick stammered.

"What -"

"Give me your gun!"

Walter drew his pistol from the holster, and

then he stepped back as Patrick snatched it away and aimed it directly at the face of Ignacious Huddlestone.

"He's one of them!" a man in the crowd shouted. "Ignacious is -"

In that moment Patrick fired, pulling the trigger six times in quick succession and sending six bullets slamming into Ignacious Huddlestone's chest. Shuddering slightly under the force of the impact, Ignacious nevertheless managed to remain standing, and he began to grin from ear to ear as the bullets slowly oozed from the wounds and dropped down harmlessly against the wooden decking.

"Lord save us!" a woman screamed.

"Pray!" Octavia shouted, dropping to her knees and clutching her hands together as she bowed her head. "It's the only way! Pray with me!"

"Do you really think that will work?" Ignacious hissed angrily. "If the Lord watched over you at all, then why would He even allow me to exist in the first place? Because that's how you see my kind, is it not? You see us as dirty and unclean, as unworthy of life or a home. We have tried so hard to make peace with your town since you arrived, especially since the mistakes made by the first Walker, but have you responded in kind? Have you made any efforts to work with us? You've barely even noticed that we exist!"

"Keep praying!" Octavia sobbed. "Don't

stop!"

"I see now that I've been wasting my time," Ignacious continued, making his way down the steps as Patrick lowered the pistol. "All these years I have spent trying to make you pathetic people understand, but you simply cannot. Soon the railroad will arrive, and then your greed will only be accelerated. There'll be nothing to constrain you, and it's my people who will suffer the consequences. But again, you don't care one iota, so long as you get your wood from our trees and your gold from our ground and -"

"It doesn't have to be like this," Patrick said firmly, interrupting him. "Now that we know, we can all work together."

"You've a naive fool," Ignacious snarled. "The history of the world is littered with the corpses of men who put their trust in others doing the right thing. You know that war is inevitable, it's just a matter of how long it takes. And now I see that perhaps putting that war off would be a mistake. Instead we need to bring it forward, to make it happen as soon as possible so that at least the wolves will stand a chance and not -"

Suddenly lunging at him, Patrick ripped the badge from his own shirt and forced it into the other man's mouth. Pushing his jaw shut, Patrick turned around and held Ignacious tight, before pressing an arm against his throat until he felt the unmistakable sensation of him swallowing the badge.

Already, the silver was fizzing and hissing as it made its way down, and Ignacious let out a gurgled cry of pain as his throat began to burn. Patrick held onto him for as long as possible, but after a few more seconds he was knocked back against the ground. Stepping forward, Ignacious clutched his chest, but his flesh was burning away as blood and steam spluttered from his lips; his eyes were bulging more than ever, and finally he dropped onto his knees as he screamed.

The gathered crowd watched in shocked silence as Ignacious began his transformation. His mouth opened wide, revealing a growing set of large fangs, but his cry continued and after a moment the front of his shirt burst open, unleashing a torrent of blood that crashed down and splattered against the ground. Frozen in place, screaming in his dying moments, Ignacious was still desperately trying to change into his wolf form even as his body burned and fell apart. He looked up at the sky, and in that moment his eyes – which had started to cook due to the heat – slowly burst and began to leak down the side of his face, while he clutched his chest and began to pull his own ribs aside in a desperate attempt to find the small piece of silver that even now was destroying him from the inside.

Finally the badge flowed out in another rush of blood, landing on the ground as Ignacious managed one final sigh and tumbled back. Before he'd even landed, his body had lost any semblance of either wolf or man and – instead – looked more like a molten pile of meat and twisted bone.

The badge, meanwhile, fizzed and skipped a little on the ground until it had burned away the puddle of flesh in which it had landed.

Slowly getting to his feet, Patrick stared in horror at the remains of Ignacious Huddlestone. For a moment he worried that the man might yet manage to reform his ruined body, but after a few seconds he began to accept that he was truly gone. And then, hearing a clapping sound, he turned to see that Octavia Willoughby was applauding him as tears ran down her face.

"Praise the Lord!" she cried out, as others joined the clapping. "We are saved!"

"Stop that," Patrick replied, disgusted by the glee he saw on the face all around him. "Don't you understand anything? He was right!"

He waited for someone to respond, but they were all shouting their thanks at the tops of their voices as if they cared only that the big bad wolf had been killed.

"He was right!" Patrick yelled again, even if now he understood that nobody could hear him. "Damn you all to Hell," he continued, "but he was right."

As the applause grew and grew, Patrick

finally began to realize that there was no way for him to persuade them. He looked around and saw so many grateful faces, yet the sight of them made him feel nauseous. He picked up the badge and briefly considered pinning it back onto his shirt, but instead he stepped over the pile of meat that had once been Ignacious Huddlestone.

Making his way along the street, he tried to ignore the people who applauded him from either side. Barely able to even meet their gazes, he slowly walked through the dirt until finally he found himself standing before the gallows. He looked up, and for a few seconds he could only stare at the corpse of Emma McShane; twisting gently in a breeze, her body was still hanging from the rope attached around her neck. Although he desperately wanted to cut her down, Patrick knew that by doing so he'd only be prolonging his time in a town that he now hated with every atom of his body.

"Bury her properly," he whispered as the applause continued, with the townsfolk now forming a circle around him.

Slowly he turned to them.

"Bury her properly!" he shouted angrily, finally causing the applause to die down. "Do you hear me?" he sneered. "If even one of you has a good honest bone left in your body, then you'll cut her down and bury her properly, in a proper grave in proper consecrated ground. You'll put a cross up... it doesn't have to be fancy, something simple will do the job, but you'll put it up and you'll make sure that it *stays* up."

Struggling to hold back tears now, he looked around at the shocked faces of the townsfolk.

"And you'll remember her name," he continued, "and you'll make sure that it's never forgotten. And you'll make sure that people understand *why* it's remembered, too. You'll do all those things and more, and you'll pick your hearts and your souls up out of the gutter, and you'll make sure that nothing like this ever happens in this town again. For all the talk of good and bad, and of right and wrong... none of it matters, not really. Not in the end. All that matters is that this..."

He pointed up at Emma's corpse.

"All that matters," he added, "is that this is never repeated. That you never kill an innocent soul ever again."

He paused, but now everyone had fallen silent and the only sound came from the creaking rope that still held Emma's body aloft. A moment later, Patrick tossed the silver badge down onto the ground beneath the set of gallows from which Emma was still hanging, and then he turned and walked over to Blackspot. Climbing up onto the horse, he took hold of the reins, and finally he road out of town, telling himself that while he had no idea where he was going next, there had to be a better place out there somewhere.

As Emma's body continued to hang from the rope, the silver badge lay on the ground in the dirt, glinting in the low light.

EPILOGUE

Today...

DEEP IN THE FOREST, several miles from the edge of town, torches burned on either side of a simple wooden walkway. The trees this far out – in a part of the region untroubled by human intervention for many centuries – were twisted and warped, with bones hanging from elaborate wires and strange carvings in a complex, ancient script.

"The Walker is here," a voice said, piercing the darkness.

A little further ahead, Saint Thomas stood in silent contemplation for a moment before turning to see that Lucian had arrived with the news.

"Finally," he murmured. "It's not often that I allow myself to be kept waiting."

As he began to make his way back along the walkway, each step rang out hard against the wooden surface.

"Why must these meetings always be conducted in human form?" Lucian asked, clearly disgusted by the whole arrangement. "Others in the pack are talking. You should know that some of them think the Walker..."

His voice trailed off for a moment.

"What do they think of the Walker?" Saint Thomas asked, stopping in front of him. "Tell me."

"Some of them," Lucian continued awkwardly, "are whispering that the Walker might have become a little... too human. That after so many years of living among them, this particular Walker has done something that none of the others would have even dared to contemplate. Some worry that *this* Walker... has begun to like them."

"You should know that such whispers are untrue," Saint Thomas said firmly.

"I want to believe that," Lucian replied, "but then I come back to the same question... why must these meetings be conducted in human form? Every single time the Walker returns with news, everything has to be done in this pathetic manner. Do you not find it strangely insulting?"

"If the Walker wants things to be like this," Saint Thomas murmured, spotting a hooded figure up ahead, "then who am I to argue? So long as I get what I want in the end, I'm happy to indulge her little eccentricities."

Stepping past Lucian, he made his way further along the walkway before stopping again just a few feet from where the Walker was standing. He watched the back of her hood, amused by her talent for intrigue and drama. In truth, he knew that many of the others were unhappy about the way the Walker conducted herself, but for his own part he was happy enough; he knew that she was reliable, and that she would always arrive swiftly with any important news from the town. He also knew that she could be rather theatrical, and he didn't mind indulging her for a few minutes whenever she deigned to show up.

On this occasion, however, he was in a little more of a hurry.

"Ahem," he said distinctly, before clearing his throat. "I don't mean to hurry you, but I kinda have a lot on right now."

He waited, but – as he'd expected – so offered no initial reply.

"Something's going to change soon," he continued. "I can feel it in my bones. I don't know *what*, exactly, but tonight's the night when something's going to... give. I'm ready for anything, though, so I'm more than happy for the universe to tilt and swivel as it wants. I'm sure as hell not gonna be put off balance."

"Don't you want to know about the pendant?" she asked, still not turning to face him.

"I guess I do," he purred.

"They can't find it," she continued. "They've been looking, they've almost turned the town upside down in the process, but they truly can't locate it anywhere. My guess is that it has been lost forever, and that their only chance now would be a miracle."

"Are you sure?"

"I've heard them discuss it myself."

"But are you *really* sure?" he asked, and now his voice betrayed no hint of humor or amusement. "We can't afford to be wrong about this. If they can defend their town -"

"They can't."

He opened his mouth to ask again if she was certain, but at the last second he held back.

"Tench and Lisa Sondnes have been searching high and low," she explained. "I've been very amused by their efforts. I confess, once or twice I even stepped in to see how things were going. Just to give myself a little levity, you understand. They tried all the obvious places, such as the church, and they also went through all the items that had been collected by our late lamented friend Joe Hicks."

"May he rest in pig shit," Saint Thomas sneered.

"The point is, they just keep coming up with

empty hands," she continued, "and I think they know that time's running out. Like you predicted, some of the other townspeople have turned against them. It's getting pretty ugly, and they're fighting each other even faster than any of us could have thought. Whatever you're planning to do next, the time has come to get on with it. Why wait any longer?"

"Indeed," he said with a smile. "Why wait?"

He watched her for a moment, wondering whether she had more to report.

"Sobolton is defenseless," she added. "For the first time in centuries, for the first time since the days of the first Walker, that filthy settlement can't fight back. We have the numbers to rip them all to pieces, so why not do it tonight? I just want to be there to see it all."

She hesitated again, before finally turning to him. She reached up, and then she slowly lowered her hood to reveal her features. Anticipation burned in her eyes and a faint smile couldn't help but creep across her lips.

"I want to be right there in the middle of it all as Sobolton burns," Carolyn continued. "And I want to hear their screams."

In this series so far:

1. Little Miss Dead
2. Swan Territory
3. Dead Widow Road
4. In a Lonely Grave
5. Electrification
6. Man on the Moon
7. Cry of the Wolf
8. In Human Bonds
9. Blood of the Lost
10. Red-Eyed Nellie
11. Echo of the Dead

Coming soon:

12. Dead End Town
13. End of the World

Next in this series

RED-EYED NELLIE
(THE HORRORS OF SOBOLTON BOOK 10)

The time has come. Blood must be spilled, and this time the wolves of Sobolton aren't going to stop until they get what they want. No-one is safe.

The Walker has finally returned to the pack after many years spent living among humans. Once the wolves have received the Walker's news, they realize that the entire town of Sobolton is defenseless. On the verge of seizing total power, Saint Thomas knows that he only has to deal with a few loose ends before he can finally achieve his destiny.

For many years, an ancient curse has held the wolves back. All Saint Thomas has to do now is make sure that this curse has been broken forever, and then he'll be able to lead his forces into Sobolton and seize the one person who might yet stand in the way of his ambitions. But has he reckoned without the fury of Lisa Sondnes? And what will happen when two formidable adversaries come face-to-face for a rematch?

Also by Amy Cross

1689
(The Haunting of Hadlow House book 1)

All Richard Hadlow wants is a happy family and a peaceful home. Having built the perfect house deep in the Kent countryside, now all he needs is a wife. He's about to discover, however, that even the most perfectly-laid plans can go horribly and tragically wrong.

The year is 1689 and England is in the grip of turmoil. A pretender is trying to take the throne, but Richard has no interest in the affairs of his country. He only cares about finding the perfect wife and giving her a perfect life. But someone – or something – at his newly-built house has other ideas. Is Richard's new life about to be destroyed forever?

Hadlow House is brand new, but already there are strange whispers in the corridors and unexplained noises at night. Has Richard been unlucky, is his new wife simply imagining things, or is a dark secret from the past about to rise up and deliver Richard's worst nightmare? Who wins when the past and the present collide?

AMY CROSS

Also by Amy Cross

The Haunting of Nelson Street
(The Ghosts of Crowford book 1)

Crowford, a sleepy coastal town in the south of England, might seem like an oasis of calm and tranquility. Beneath the surface, however, dark secrets are waiting to claim fresh victims, and ghostly figures plot revenge.

Having finally decided to leave the hustle of London, Daisy and Richard Johnson buy two houses on Nelson Street, a picturesque street in the center of Crowford. One house is perfect and ready to move into, while the other is a fire-ravaged wreck that needs a lot of work. They figure they have plenty of time to work on the damaged house while Daisy recovers from a traumatic event.

Soon, they discover that the two houses share a common link to the past. Something awful once happened on Nelson Street, something that shook the town to its core.

Also by Amy Cross

The Revenge of the Mercy Belle
(The Ghosts of Crowford book 2)

The year is 1950, and a great tragedy has struck the town of Crowford. Three local men have been killed in a storm, after their fishing boat the Mercy Belle sank. A mysterious fourth man, however, was rescue. Nobody knows who he is, or what he was doing on the Mercy Belle... and the man has lost his memory.

Five years later, messages from the dead warn of impending doom for Crowford. The ghosts of the Mercy Belle's crew demand revenge, and the whole town is being punished. The fourth man still has no memory of his previous existence, but he's married now and living under the named Edward Smith. As Crowford's suffering continues, the locals begin to turn against him.

What really happened on the night the Mercy Belle sank? Did the fourth man cause the tragedy? And will Crowford survive if this man is not sent to meet his fate?

AMY CROSS

Also by Amy Cross

The Devil, the Witch and the Whore
(The Deal book 1)

"Leave the forest alone. Whatever's out there, just let it be. Don't make it angry."

When a horrific discovery is made at the edge of town, Sheriff James Kopperud realizes the answers he seeks might be waiting beyond in the vast forest. But everybody in the town of Deal knows that there's something out there in the forest, something that should never be disturbed. A deal was made long ago, a deal that was supposed to keep the town safe. And if he insists on investigating the murder of a local girl, James is going to have to break that deal and head out into the wilderness.

Meanwhile, James has no idea that his estranged daughter Ramsey has returned to town. Ramsey is running from something, and she thinks she can find safety in the vast tunnel system that runs beneath the forest. Before long, however, Ramsey finds herself coming face to face with creatures that hide in the shadows. One of these creatures is known as the devil, and another is known as the witch. They're both waiting for the whore to arrive, but for very different reasons. And soon Ramsey is offered a terrible deal, one that could save or destroy the entire town, and maybe even the world.

Also by Amy Cross

If You Didn't Like Me Then, You Probably Won't Like Me Now

One year ago, Sheryl and her friends did something bad. Really bad. They ritually humiliated local girl Rachel Ritter, before posting the video online for all to see. After that night, Rachel left town and was never seen again. Until now.

Late one night, Sheryl and her friends realize that Rachel's back. At first they think there's on reason to be concerned, but a series of strange events soon convince them that they need to be worried. On the outside, Rachel acts as if all is forgiven, but she's hiding a shocking secret that soon starts to have deadly consequences.

By the time they understand the full horror of Rachel's plans, Sheryl and her friends might be too late to save themselves. Is Rachel really out for revenge? What does she have in store for her tormentors? And just how far is she willing to go? Would she, for example, do something that nobody in all of human history has ever managed to achieve?

If You Didn't Like Me Then, You Probably Won't Like Me Now is a horror novel about the surprising nature of revenge, about the power of hatred, and about the future of humanity.

Also by Amy Cross

The Soul Auction

"I saw a woman on the beach. I watched her face a demon."

Thirty years after her mother's death, Alice Ashcroft is drawn back to the coastal English town of Curridge. Somebody in Curridge has been reviewing Alice's novels online, and in those reviews there have been tantalizing hints at a hidden truth. A truth that seems to be linked to her dead mother.

"Thirty years ago, there was a soul auction."

Once she reaches Curridge, Alice finds strange things happening all around her. Something attacks her car. A figure watches her on the beach at night. And when she tries to find the person who has been reviewing her books, she makes a horrific discovery.

What really happened to Alice's mother thirty years ago? Who was she talking to, just moments before dropping dead on the beach? What caused a huge rockfall that nearly tore a nearby cliff-face in half? And what sinister presence is lurking in the grounds of the local church?

Also by Amy Cross

American Coven

He kidnapped three women and held them in his basement. He thought they couldn't fight back. He was wrong...

Snatched from the street near her home, Holly Carter is taken to a rural house and thrown down into a stone basement. She meets two other women who have also been kidnapped, and soon Holly learns about the horrific rituals that take place in the house. Eventually, she's called upstairs to take her place in the ice bath.

As her nightmare continues, however, Holly learns about a mysterious power that exists in the basement, and which the three women might be able to harness. When they finally manage to get through the metal door, however, the women have no idea that their fight for freedom is going to stretch out for more than a decade, or that it will culminate in a final, devastating demonstration of their new-found powers.

Also by Amy Cross

The Ash House

Why would anyone ever return to a haunted house?

For Diane Mercer the answer is simple. She's dying of cancer, and she wants to know once and for all whether ghosts are real.

Heading home with her young son, Diane is determined to find out whether the stories are real. After all, everyone else claimed to see and hear strange things in the house over the years. Everyone except Diane had some kind of experience in the house, or in the little ash house in the yard.

As Diane explores the house where she grew up, however, her son is exploring the yard and the forest. And while his mother might be struggling to come to terms with her own impending death, Daniel Mercer is puzzled by fleeting appearances of a strange little girl who seems drawn to the ash house, and by strange, rasping coughs that he keeps hearing at night.

The Ash House is a horror novel about a woman who desperately wants to know what will happen to her when she dies, and about a boy who uncovers the shocking truth about a young girl's murder.

Also by Amy Cross

Haunted

Twenty years ago, the ghost of a dead little girl drove Sheriff Michael Blaine to his death.

Now, that same ghost is coming for his daughter.

Returning to the small town where she grew up, Alex Roberts is determined to live a normal, quiet life. For the residents of Railham, however, she's an unwelcome reminder of the town's darkest hour.

Twenty years ago, nine-year-old Mo Garvey was found brutally murdered in a nearby forest. Everyone thinks that Alex's father was responsible, but if the killer was brought to justice, why is the ghost of Mo Garvey still after revenge?

And how far will the real killer go to protect his secret, when Alex starts getting closer to the truth?

Haunted is a horror novel about a woman who has to face her past, about a town that would rather forget, and about a little girl who refuses to let death stand in her way.

AMY CROSS

Also by Amy Cross

The Curse of Wetherley House

"If you walk through that door, Evil Mary will get you."

When she agrees to visit a supposedly haunted house with an old friend, Rosie assumes she'll encounter nothing more scary than a few creaks and bumps in the night. Even the legend of Evil Mary doesn't put her off. After all, she knows ghosts aren't real. But when Mary makes her first appearance, Rosie realizes she might already be trapped.

For more than a century, Wetherley House has been cursed. A horrific encounter on a remote road in the late 1800's has already caused a chain of misery and pain for all those who live at the house. Wetherley House was abandoned long ago, after a terrible discovery in the basement, something has remained undetected within its room. And even the local children know that Evil Mary waits in the house for anyone foolish enough to walk through the front door.

Before long, Rosie realizes that her entire life has been defined by the spirit of a woman who died in agony. Can she become the first person to escape Evil Mary, or will she fall victim to the same fate as the house's other occupants?

AMY CROSS

BOOKS BY AMY CROSS

1. Dark Season: The Complete First Series (2011)
2. Werewolves of Soho (Lupine Howl book 1) (2012)
3. Werewolves of the Other London (Lupine Howl book 2) (2012)
4. Ghosts: The Complete Series (2012)
5. Dark Season: The Complete Second Series (2012)
6. The Children of Black Annis (Lupine Howl book 3) (2012)
7. Destiny of the Last Wolf (Lupine Howl book 4) (2012)
8. Asylum (The Asylum Trilogy book 1) (2012)
9. Dark Season: The Complete Third Series (2013)
10. Devil's Briar (2013)
11. Broken Blue (The Broken Trilogy book 1) (2013)
12. The Night Girl (2013)
13. Days 1 to 4 (Mass Extinction Event book 1) (2013)
14. Days 5 to 8 (Mass Extinction Event book 2) (2013)
15. The Library (The Library Chronicles book 1) (2013)
16. American Coven (2013)
17. Werewolves of Sangreth (Lupine Howl book 5) (2013)
18. Broken White (The Broken Trilogy book 2) (2013)
19. Grave Girl (Grave Girl book 1) (2013)
20. Other People's Bodies (2013)
21. The Shades (2013)
22. The Vampire's Grave and Other Stories (2013)
23. Darper Danver: The Complete First Series (2013)
24. The Hollow Church (2013)
25. The Dead and the Dying (2013)
26. Days 9 to 16 (Mass Extinction Event book 3) (2013)
27. The Girl Who Never Came Back (2013)
28. Ward Z (The Ward Z Series book 1) (2013)
29. Journey to the Library (The Library Chronicles book 2) (2014)
30. The Vampires of Tor Cliff Asylum (2014)
31. The Family Man (2014)
32. The Devil's Blade (2014)
33. The Immortal Wolf (Lupine Howl book 6) (2014)
34. The Dying Streets (Detective Laura Foster book 1) (2014)
35. The Stars My Home (2014)
36. The Ghost in the Rain and Other Stories (2014)
37. Ghosts of the River Thames (The Robinson Chronicles book 1) (2014)
38. The Wolves of Cur'eath (2014)
39. Days 46 to 53 (Mass Extinction Event book 4) (2014)
40. The Man Who Saw the Face of the World (2014)
41. The Art of Dying (Detective Laura Foster book 2) (2014)
42. Raven Revivals (Grave Girl book 2) (2014)

AMY CROSS

43. Arrival on Thaxos (Dead Souls book 1) (2014)
44. Birthright (Dead Souls book 2) (2014)
45. A Man of Ghosts (Dead Souls book 3) (2014)
46. The Haunting of Hardstone Jail (2014)
47. A Very Respectable Woman (2015)
48. Better the Devil (2015)
49. The Haunting of Marshall Heights (2015)
50. Terror at Camp Everbee (The Ward Z Series book 2) (2015)
51. Guided by Evil (Dead Souls book 4) (2015)
52. Child of a Bloodied Hand (Dead Souls book 5) (2015)
53. Promises of the Dead (Dead Souls book 6) (2015)
54. Days 54 to 61 (Mass Extinction Event book 5) (2015)
55. Angels in the Machine (The Robinson Chronicles book 2) (2015)
56. The Curse of Ah-Qal's Tomb (2015)
57. Broken Red (The Broken Trilogy book 3) (2015)
58. The Farm (2015)
59. Fallen Heroes (Detective Laura Foster book 3) (2015)
60. The Haunting of Emily Stone (2015)
61. Cursed Across Time (Dead Souls book 7) (2015)
62. Destiny of the Dead (Dead Souls book 8) (2015)
63. The Death of Jennifer Kazakos (Dead Souls book 9) (2015)
64. Alice Isn't Well (Death Herself book 1) (2015)
65. Annie's Room (2015)
66. The House on Everley Street (Death Herself book 2) (2015)
67. Meds (The Asylum Trilogy book 2) (2015)
68. Take Me to Church (2015)
69. Ascension (Demon's Grail book 1) (2015)
70. The Priest Hole (Nykolas Freeman book 1) (2015)
71. Eli's Town (2015)
72. The Horror of Raven's Briar Orphanage (Dead Souls book 10) (2015)
73. The Witch of Thaxos (Dead Souls book 11) (2015)
74. The Rise of Ashalla (Dead Souls book 12) (2015)
75. Evolution (Demon's Grail book 2) (2015)
76. The Island (The Island book 1) (2015)
77. The Lighthouse (2015)
78. The Cabin (The Cabin Trilogy book 1) (2015)
79. At the Edge of the Forest (2015)
80. The Devil's Hand (2015)
81. The 13th Demon (Demon's Grail book 3) (2016)
82. After the Cabin (The Cabin Trilogy book 2) (2016)
83. The Border: The Complete Series (2016)
84. The Dead Ones (Death Herself book 3) (2016)
85. A House in London (2016)
86. Persona (The Island book 2) (2016)

87. Battlefield (Nykolas Freeman book 2) (2016)
88. Perfect Little Monsters and Other Stories (2016)
89. The Ghost of Shapley Hall (2016)
90. The Blood House (2016)
91. The Death of Addie Gray (2016)
92. The Girl With Crooked Fangs (2016)
93. Last Wrong Turn (2016)
94. The Body at Auercliff (2016)
95. The Printer From Hell (2016)
96. The Dog (2016)
97. The Nurse (2016)
98. The Haunting of Blackwych Grange (2016)
99. Twisted Little Things and Other Stories (2016)
100. The Horror of Devil's Root Lake (2016)
101. The Disappearance of Katie Wren (2016)
102. B&B (2016)
103. The Bride of Ashbyrn House (2016)
104. The Devil, the Witch and the Whore (The Deal Trilogy book 1) (2016)
105. The Ghosts of Lakeforth Hotel (2016)
106. The Ghost of Longthorn Manor and Other Stories (2016)
107. Laura (2017)
108. The Murder at Skellin Cottage (Jo Mason book 1) (2017)
109. The Curse of Wetherley House (2017)
110. The Ghosts of Hexley Airport (2017)
111. The Return of Rachel Stone (Jo Mason book 2) (2017)
112. Haunted (2017)
113. The Vampire of Downing Street and Other Stories (2017)
114. The Ash House (2017)
115. The Ghost of Molly Holt (2017)
116. The Camera Man (2017)
117. The Soul Auction (2017)
118. The Abyss (The Island book 3) (2017)
119. Broken Window (The House of Jack the Ripper book 1) (2017)
120. In Darkness Dwell (The House of Jack the Ripper book 2) (2017)
121. Cradle to Grave (The House of Jack the Ripper book 3) (2017)
122. The Lady Screams (The House of Jack the Ripper book 4) (2017)
123. A Beast Well Tamed (The House of Jack the Ripper book 5) (2017)
124. Doctor Charles Grazier (The House of Jack the Ripper book 6) (2017)
125. The Raven Watcher (The House of Jack the Ripper book 7) (2017)
126. The Final Act (The House of Jack the Ripper book 8) (2017)
127. Stephen (2017)
128. The Spider (2017)
129. The Mermaid's Revenge (2017)
130. The Girl Who Threw Rocks at the Devil (2018)

AMY CROSS

131. Friend From the Internet (2018)
132. Beautiful Familiar (2018)
133. One Night at a Soul Auction (2018)
134. 16 Frames of the Devil's Face (2018)
135. The Haunting of Caldgrave House (2018)
136. Like Stones on a Crow's Back (The Deal Trilogy book 2) (2018)
137. Room 9 and Other Stories (2018)
138. The Gravest Girl of All (Grave Girl book 3) (2018)
139. Return to Thaxos (Dead Souls book 13) (2018)
140. The Madness of Annie Radford (The Asylum Trilogy book 3) (2018)
141. The Haunting of Briarwych Church (Briarwych book 1) (2018)
142. I Just Want You To Be Happy (2018)
143. Day 100 (Mass Extinction Event book 6) (2018)
144. The Horror of Briarwych Church (Briarwych book 2) (2018)
145. The Ghost of Briarwych Church (Briarwych book 3) (2018)
146. Lights Out (2019)
147. Apocalypse (The Ward Z Series book 3) (2019)
148. Days 101 to 108 (Mass Extinction Event book 7) (2019)
149. The Haunting of Daniel Bayliss (2019)
150. The Purchase (2019)
151. Harper's Hotel Ghost Girl (Death Herself book 4) (2019)
152. The Haunting of Aldburn House (2019)
153. Days 109 to 116 (Mass Extinction Event book 8) (2019)
154. Bad News (2019)
155. The Wedding of Rachel Blaine (2019)
156. Dark Little Wonders and Other Stories (2019)
157. The Music Man (2019)
158. The Vampire Falls (Three Nights of the Vampire book 1) (2019)
159. The Other Ann (2019)
160. The Butcher's Husband and Other Stories (2019)
161. The Haunting of Lannister Hall (2019)
162. The Vampire Burns (Three Nights of the Vampire book 2) (2019)
163. Days 195 to 202 (Mass Extinction Event book 9) (2019)
164. Escape From Hotel Necro (2019)
165. The Vampire Rises (Three Nights of the Vampire book 3) (2019)
166. Ten Chimes to Midnight: A Collection of Ghost Stories (2019)
167. The Strangler's Daughter (2019)
168. The Beast on the Tracks (2019)
169. The Haunting of the King's Head (2019)
170. I Married a Serial Killer (2019)
171. Your Inhuman Heart (2020)
172. Days 203 to 210 (Mass Extinction Event book 10) (2020)
173. The Ghosts of David Brook (2020)
174. Days 349 to 356 (Mass Extinction Event book 11) (2020)

175. The Horror at Criven Farm (2020)
176. Mary (2020)
177. The Middlewych Experiment (Chaos Gear Annie book 1) (2020)
178. Days 357 to 364 (Mass Extinction Event book 12) (2020)
179. Day 365: The Final Day (Mass Extinction Event book 13) (2020)
180. The Haunting of Hathaway House (2020)
181. Don't Let the Devil Know Your Name (2020)
182. The Legend of Rinth (2020)
183. The Ghost of Old Coal House (2020)
184. The Root (2020)
185. I'm Not a Zombie (2020)
186. The Ghost of Annie Close (2020)
187. The Disappearance of Lonnie James (2020)
188. The Curse of the Langfords (2020)
189. The Haunting of Nelson Street (The Ghosts of Crowford 1) (2020)
190. Strange Little Horrors and Other Stories (2020)
191. The House Where She Died (2020)
192. The Revenge of the Mercy Belle (The Ghosts of Crowford 2) (2020)
193. The Ghost of Crowford School (The Ghosts of Crowford book 3) (2020)
194. The Haunting of Hardlocke House (2020)
195. The Cemetery Ghost (2020)
196. You Should Have Seen Her (2020)
197. The Portrait of Sister Elsa (The Ghosts of Crowford book 4) (2021)
198. The House on Fisher Street (2021)
199. The Haunting of the Crowford Hoy (The Ghosts of Crowford 5) (2021)
200. Trill (2021)
201. The Horror of the Crowford Empire (The Ghosts of Crowford 6) (2021)
202. Out There (The Ted Armitage Trilogy book 1) (2021)
203. The Nightmare of Crowford Hospital (The Ghosts of Crowford 7) (2021)
204. Twist Valley (The Ted Armitage Trilogy book 2) (2021)
205. The Great Beyond (The Ted Armitage Trilogy book 3) (2021)
206. The Haunting of Edward House (2021)
207. The Curse of the Crowford Grand (The Ghosts of Crowford 8) (2021)
208. How to Make a Ghost (2021)
209. The Ghosts of Crossley Manor (The Ghosts of Crowford 9) (2021)
210. The Haunting of Matthew Thorne (2021)
211. The Siege of Crowford Castle (The Ghosts of Crowford 10) (2021)
212. Daisy: The Complete Series (2021)
213. Bait (Bait book 1) (2021)
214. Origin (Bait book 2) (2021)
215. Heretic (Bait book 3) (2021)
216. Anna's Sister (2021)
217. The Haunting of Quist House (The Rose Files 1) (2021)
218. The Haunting of Crowford Station (The Ghosts of Crowford 11) (2022)

AMY CROSS

219. The Curse of Rosie Stone (2022)
220. The First Order (The Chronicles of Sister June book 1) (2022)
221. The Second Veil (The Chronicles of Sister June book 2) (2022)
222. The Graves of Crowford Rise (The Ghosts of Crowford 12) (2022)
223. Dead Man: The Resurrection of Morton Kane (2022)
224. The Third Beast (The Chronicles of Sister June book 3) (2022)
225. The Legend of the Crossley Stag (The Ghosts of Crowford 13) (2022)
226. One Star (2022)
227. The Ghost in Room 119 (2022)
228. The Fourth Shadow (The Chronicles of Sister June book 4) (2022)
229. The Soldier Without a Past (Dead Souls book 14) (2022)
230. The Ghosts of Marsh House (2022)
231. Wax: The Complete Series (2022)
232. The Phantom of Crowford Theatre (The Ghosts of Crowford 14) (2022)
233. The Haunting of Hurst House (Mercy Willow book 1) (2022)
234. Blood Rains Down From the Sky (The Deal Trilogy book 3) (2022)
235. The Spirit on Sidle Street (Mercy Willow book 2) (2022)
236. The Ghost of Gower Grange (Mercy Willow book 3) (2022)
237. The Curse of Clute Cottage (Mercy Willow book 4) (2022)
238. The Haunting of Anna Jenkins (Mercy Willow book 5) (2023)
239. The Death of Mercy Willow (Mercy Willow book 6) (2023)
240. Angel (2023)
241. The Eyes of Maddy Park (2023)
242. If You Didn't Like Me Then, You Probably Won't Like Me Now (2023)
243. The Terror of Torfork Tower (Mercy Willow 7) (2023)
244. The Phantom of Payne Priory (Mercy Willow 8) (2023)
245. The Devil on Davis Drive (Mercy Willow 9) (2023)
246. The Haunting of the Ghost of Tom Bell (Mercy Willow 10) (2023)
247. The Other Ghost of Gower Grange (Mercy Willow 11) (2023)
248. The Haunting of Olive Atkins (Mercy Willow 12) (2023)
249. The End of Marcy Willow (Mercy Willow 13) (2023)
250. The Last Haunted House on Mars and Other Stories (2023)
251. 1689 (The Haunting of Hadlow House 1) (2023)
252. 1722 (The Haunting of Hadlow House 2) (2023)
253. 1775 (The Haunting of Hadlow House 3) (2023)
254. The Terror of Crowford Carnival (The Ghosts of Crowford 15) (2023)
255. 1800 (The Haunting of Hadlow House 4) (2023)
256. 1837 (The Haunting of Hadlow House 5) (2023)
257. 1885 (The Haunting of Hadlow House 6) (2023)
258. 1901 (The Haunting of Hadlow House 7) (2023)
259. 1918 (The Haunting of Hadlow House 8) (2023)
260. The Secret of Adam Grey (The Ghosts of Crowford 16) (2023)
261. 1926 (The Haunting of Hadlow House 9) (2023)
262. 1939 (The Haunting of Hadlow House 10) (2023)

263. The Fifth Tomb (The Chronicles of Sister June 5) (2023)
264. 1966 (The Haunting of Hadlow House 11) (2023)
265. 1999 (The Haunting of Hadlow House 12) (2023)
266. The Hauntings of Mia Rush (2023)
267. 2024 (The Haunting of Hadlow House 13) (2024)
268. The Sixth Window (The Chronicles of Sister June 6) (2024)
269. Little Miss Dead (The Horrors of Sobolton 1) (2024)
270. Swan Territory (The Horrors of Sobolton 2) (2024)
271. Dead Widow Road (The Horrors of Sobolton 3) (2024)
272. The Haunting of Stryke Brothers (The Ghosts of Crowford 17) (2024)
273. In a Lonely Grave (The Horrors of Sobolton 4) (2024)
274. Electrification (The Horrors of Sobolton 5) (2024)
275. Man on the Moon (The Horrors of Sobolton 6) (2024)
276. The Haunting of Styre House (The Smythe Trilogy book 1) (2024)
277. The Curse of Bloodacre Farm (The Smythe Trilogy book 2) (2024)
278. The Horror of Styre House (The Smythe Trilogy book 3) (2024)
279. Cry of the Wolf (The Horrors of Sobolton book 7) (2024)
280. A Cuckoo in Winter (2024)
281. The Ghost of Harry Prym (2024)
282. In Human Bonds (The Horrors of Sobolton book 8) (2024)
283. Here & Now (The Duchess of Zombie Street book 1) (2024)
284. Blood & Bone (The Duchess of Zombie Street book 2) (2024)
285. Dust & Rain (The Duchess of Zombie Street book 3) (2024)
286. Hope & Hail (The Duchess of Zombie Street book 4) (2024)
287. Blood of the Lost (The Horrors of Sobolton book 9) (2024)

AMY CROSS

For more information, visit:

www.amycross.com

AMY CROSS

Printed in Great Britain
by Amazon